Dear Hayley,

I hope you enjoy the book!

Ela Lou

DRAGON BORN

Ela Lourenco

Sirens Call Publications

Dragon Born

Print Edition; First Edition

Edited by Gloria Bobrowicz

Cover Design © Sirens Call Publications

ISBN-13: 978-0692380482 (Sirens Call Publications)
ISBN-10: 0692380485

DEDICATION

For my beautiful daughters, Larissa and Asena, and my beloved nieces Leyla and Sofia. You each inspire me daily with every little thing you do and say. Your enjoyment in reading these books are what keeps me motivated.

DRAGON BORN

ACKNOWLEDGEMENTS

There are so many people to thank it is impossible to mention them all. But special thanks to my family. To my husband Paulo and daughters Larissa and Asena, for their unwavering support (also to my hubby for his invaluable IT support!!) To my mother Leyla for her lifelong encouragement and for infecting me with the love of reading and writing (you are also the reason for my huge kindle bills!) To my father Ferit, my brother Hakan, my sister-in-law Lidia who is a true sister, and my beautiful nieces Leyla and Sofia I give thanks for all their love and enthusiasm.

I would like to give special thanks to my young friend Libby Simpson who has read all of my young adult books to date and given valuable feedback and support. Thanks also to Libby and Anna Simpson for lending their 'names' to my characters!

I would also like to acknowledge the hard work put in by the whole Sirens Call Publications team. Thank you for enjoying my book. Thank you for putting up with my endless questions and emails! A most particular thank you to Gloria (Bobrowicz), Editor-in-Chief at Sirens Call Publications. You have been amazing, the support you have given me has been tremendous (to the point that I have often wondered when and if you sleep!!) Nina (D'Arcangela)—you are amazing—always capturing what I have in my head just right! And Julianne (Snow)—you are always one email away with ready answers and support. I am truly fortunate that such a team of strong and creative women have my back.

This book has been a true labour of love, born of my eldest daughter's request for me to write a book that was appropriate for her age! I have enjoyed every second of it (and the other four books that will follow in the Dragon Born series!)

Thank you and I hope you all enjoy my story.

PROLOGUE

In the universe, on a different dimension from Earth, is a world called Azmantium. It is a planet with lilac skies, jade green seas and two red fiery suns. Many people live on Azmantium, people not so different to you or me... except that they are all magical beings. Everything on this planet works with magic, from the tides of the sea to the centre of gravity. Everyone here is born with magic and powers, although some are more powerful than others. And of course, like on Earth, there is a constant struggle between good and evil...

LOST PROPHECY
DRACONIS 1116 BEW(BEFORE END OF WAR)

In ancient times it came to pass
A surface peace that could not last
For eons it was kill and die
Until one fought to unify.
The dark is never far behind
Like calls to like, seeks its own kind
Dragon-born will lead the way
Two halves of a whole to save the day
To save it or to end it be
That is up to followed destiny
To conquer; must end at the start
To calm the beast's raging heart.

CHAPTER 1

The sky was dark, not a star in sight as the woman glided through the deserted streets. Her feet barely touched the ground as she silently made her way to the back door of the small stone house at the end of the street. She paused and looked at the house. She had been searching for the right place for many years. This small but welcoming house, with its red stone walls and silvery slate roof, spoke to something inside of her. This was where she would leave her precious cargo.

She rang the doorbell and waited. A petite woman she knew to be called Yelena answered the door with a warm smile, her green eyes twinkling in the soft light of the porch.

"Good evening. Can I help you?" Yelena asked.

The woman slid her hood back slightly so Yelena could see her face.

"Gods above!" Yelena gasped as she looked at the beautiful blonde woman radiating light from her very pores. A tattoo in the shape of a flame was etched on her right cheek leaving no doubts as to her identity. "Please come in!"

The woman followed her into the living room and sat gingerly on the end of one of the large comfortable armchairs as she looked around with interest. Yelena sat opposite her, still speechless, and waited for her guest to talk.

"I can see that you recognise me," the woman began. "That is good... too many have forgotten the old ways... I am here on a matter of the utmost importance. I need your help. What I will ask of you will be a great burden to you and will bring grave danger to you and those around you..." she trailed off and looked at Yelena as though assessing her.

Yelena nodded. "It is an honour my lady... I did not think I would ever meet you... no one even knows you truly exist."

The woman nodded. "And that is how it must remain. There are those who have sought to exterminate us from the face of this world. If they were to find out the truth no one would be safe."

Yelena bowed her head respectfully. "What is it that I can do my lady?"

The woman took a large blue egg from under her heavy cloak.

"Is that what I think it is?" Yelena gasped.

The woman nodded. "It is the very last of its kind Yelena. I have kept it safe and hidden in magical stasis for many a year, but now it is time. It is time for the dawning of a new era." She put the egg in Yelena's hands, it was warm to the touch. "You must take care of it for all our sakes... and no matter what happens, no one must ever know the truth until the time is right."

Yelena hugged the egg against her chest. "I will not fail you my lady. Will I see you again?"

The woman nodded. "Our paths will cross again... until then, keep safe."

Yelena watched the woman pull her hood back on as she left the house and gracefully glided away into the darkness. She *cradled the egg in her arms as she warded the door with her earth magicks—she would have to be very careful if she was to succeed in her mission.*

Lara paced her room excitedly as she waited for the red sun to rise. She absentmindedly brushed her chestnut hair for the hundredth time as she stared out of the window impatiently as if that would scare the sun into speeding up its ascent into the sky. She was already dressed, ready for her first day at the Lantis School of Magic. She had been ready for hours already, and changed clothes at least a dozen times. The first glimmer of lilac filtered in through the window as the dark purple night sky receded. Finally! She grabbed her bag and almost ran into her foster mother Yelena, as she swung the door open.

"Sorry Yelena!!"

The older woman chuckled, "Someone's excited for her first day!"

Lara smiled, her blue eyes twinkling. "I have been waiting for today for forever!"

Yelena laughed, her eyes crinkling up. "Oh yes, seeing as you're so old at twelve, I can see that you've had a terrible wait! Just joking, I remember how excited I was when I started magic school..."

"Yes, yes," Lara rolled her eyes, "you've told me all about how you aced all your exams and were the exemplary student... although that's not what I hear from Aunt Aelwen. She told me that you were the leader of the troublemaker pack!" She dodged aside as Yelena laughingly tried to swat her.

"Think of all the spells I'm going to learn, and all the potions! And I'm finally going to get tested!! I can't wait to know what my powers are!!" Lara grabbed a banana muffin off the kitchen table and took a big bite as Yelena poured her a glass of milk.

"What do you think my powers will be?" Lara asked between gulps of milk. "Do you think I will have earth magicks like you?"

"Honey, I wish you would sit down to have your breakfast, you're going to get indigestion! And I don't know what power you will get. Don't worry you will find out soon enough." Yelena looked worried as she busied herself at the sink. "Honey, I know you're excited, and you should be, but promise me you'll be careful at the testing... don't overuse your power or try too hard... remember you get retested every year and only your final test will count when you graduate at eighteen. This test is just to get an idea of which area your power lies."

Lara shrugged, "I know but I want to do well. Besides, you said that the test is completely safe, and Aunt Aelwen is going to be there anyway."

Yelena smiled, "Yes, she is. But you must remember not to call her that at school. You have to call her Miss Ville or Elder Aelwen like all the other students."

Lara nodded as she put her plate and cup next to the sink. Aelwen wasn't her real aunt, more like an honorary one due to her being Yelena's best friend. Aelwen was the headmistress of the Lantis School of Magic as well as being one of the five Elders on the elected Council of Azmantium which answered directly to King Merrick, and ensured the safe and legal use of magic- a type of police, government and justice system all rolled into one. The council also ran all the magic schools across Azmantium and was responsible for the testing and registration of all students. Lara's foster mother Yelena ran one of Lantis's foster homes and she and Aelwen had been friends since they met at magic school many years ago.

Elders were chosen for life by the other elders on the committee and they were always selected from the most powerful beings in Azmantium. They had to be a registered level five, the highest level ever recorded in the history of Lantis. Very few people ever registered above a level two, three was already considered to be a high level. Yelena was a level three fae sorceress which meant that she had a very strong connection with the magic of the earth. Children often had similar magicks to their parents although magical power was not necessarily hereditary and a child could have more or less power (and a different power) than his parents. For this reason, the tests administered at the magic schools were important- they were essential to find out where each child's powers belonged and where they would be placed upon graduation. The higher powered members of each race were usually recruited into the council in various roles depending on the nature of their powers. There were healers, psychics, and protectors... different roles for different skills. Aelwen was a level five witch, and she had two powers (most people only had one); illusion and pyro kinesis- two very rare and important powers. She also happened to be the third most powerful being in Lantis, after Akkarin the head of the elders who had the powers of replica (temporarily having the ability to copy another's powers) and mind control, and of course the

King, Merrick, who was the most powerful of them all. Lara had never met any of the other elders but everyone knew all about them, and if she was lucky she would eventually meet more of them, maybe if she was good enough she might even get to be taught by them.

Lara smiled as Talia, another resident of the Lantis Home for Orphans, came into the kitchen. Talia grumbled good-naturedly as Lara ruffled her hair and dropped a kiss on her head.

"Lara you are so lucky!" she bounced up and down excitedly on her little legs. "I can't wait 'til I'm twelve and I can go too!!"

"Oh honey, youɪ turn will come," Yelena smiled.

"You only have six years to wait," Lara winked. "And then watch out everyone... there will be a new troublemaker in town!"

Talia pouted. "I hate that I'm only six... I wish there was a potion to make me grow up faster!"

"I promise if I find such a potion I will bring it straight to you." Lara ruffled her hair.

Talia leapt onto her and buried her little face into Lara's stomach. "I'm going to miss you so much," her eyes filled with tears. "Who's going to play float the bubble with me when you're gone?"

"Emmy or Sadie will play with you," Lara consoled her, "and I'm only going to be staying there on weekdays, you'll see me every weekend."

Talia nodded solemnly. "I'll still miss you... and Emmy and Sadie don't let me win when we play."

Lara said her goodbyes to Yelena and the rest of the orphanage family. Emmy, Sadie, Talia and Lara were the sum total of the residents at the home. There were other larger orphanages in Lantis and at one point Yelena had had up to ten girls living with her, but that was before Lara's time. Lara had once asked her why she had so few charges and Yelena had told her that she preferred to have fewer kids as it made it feel more like a real family. Yelena had been married once but her husband had died and they had had no children of their own—that was how she came to open a home for girls.

Despite having looked forward to going to magic school Lara felt a sharp stab of sorrow as she walked down the hallway to get her bag. She looked around her room as if seeing it for the first time. The cheery blue walls were dotted with photos and pictures of her sisters at the home and the large mahogany shelves were crammed with an assortment of books and ornaments she had collected over the years. She stuffed the good luck card the girls had made for her into her bag. Saying goodbye to the girls she considered her sisters was harder than she had thought it would be—even though she would see them every weekend, she felt a little as if her whole world was about to change.

She was finally going to learn proper magic, not just party tricks like getting the dishes to wash themselves or changing the colour of your dress, she was going to learn the real stuff. She hugged herself excitedly, this time tomorrow she would know what magic caste she belonged to and what magical careers would be available to her when she graduated. Everyone went to magic school between the ages of twelve to eighteen. The Council had ruled long ago that it was better not to expose children under twelve to magical learning- for their own safety but also for the safety of others. Casting spells and mixing potions wasn't all fairy dust and rainbows... it could get dangerous, particularly so in the hands of adventurous young children. Some Council advisors also believed that using too much magic before coming of age could cause certain negative effects. Aunt Aelwen had explained all this to Lara last year when she had begged and pleaded to be sent to magic school early. She was a kind witch and managed to talk to her about the importance of being emotionally ready as well as physically without making her feel like she was being lectured. Yelena had compromised and agreed that she could go when she was twelve... the last year had gone by so slowly! Each day lasted an eternity as she counted down the days.

Yelena gave her a hug and a kiss as Lara walked towards the door. "Good luck sweetheart, I'll keep my fingers crossed that you enjoy your first day. I'm going to miss you so much!"

Lara smiled at Yelena, the only mother she had ever known, "I know I'm going to love it. I can feel it! I'll miss you too, but I will be home at the weekends."

Lara waved at Yelena and the girls as she took her seat in the craft the school had sent to get her. She watched the world under her whizz by as the craft lifted off the ground. She loved flying, and soon she would have her own licence and be allowed to fly by herself. She had been saving up to buy herself a broom, and had already picked out a gorgeous dark purple broom at the shop. Beautifully hand -carved out of shiny Jamaya wood. It wasn't one of the newer super-fast light weight models and it didn't have the autopilot flight mode spell but it was the one she wanted.

The craft finally came to a stop in front of the most imposing building. The Lantis School of Magic was an old building made completely out of silver stone. It gleamed in the red light of the sun, enormous and proud as if it were the centre of the universe. The one cavernous door and multitude of windows were all hand crafted out of Rama wood, the most expensive and rarest wood on Azmantium because it only grew in a few parts of the planet. Lara stood in front of the school, staring up at it in awe. She had seen it many times in her life, had flown past it almost daily on her way to her last school, and yet it felt as if she had never seen it before. There was a majesty about the place, as if it were alive.

"Make your way to the main hall now, they'll be waiting for you," the driver said to her and the rest of the kids on the bus.

Lara looked around her, she had barely noticed the others on the bus so lost was she in her own thoughts. They all looked as nervous as she felt. A kind looking girl smiled at her openly as she walked towards the front door.

CHAPTER 2

Lara took a deep breath to steady her nerves and walked up the long row of stairs to the door. Just as she was about to open the door someone crashed into her from behind, knocking her bag off her shoulder and all its contents onto the floor.

"Oh no! I'm so sorry! Let me help you with that," exclaimed a blond girl. "Oh dear. That wasn't how I was planning on starting my first day here... so sorry. I didn't wake up in time this morning and then I got juice on my clothes so I had to change. Then when I was finally ready and waiting on the broom, my mum remembered that she had forgotten her documents at home... well, it took her forever to find them and by then we had to rush here and well... I was just running up the stairs and I kind of saw you but by then it was too late and I couldn't stop in time... I am rambling on and on, and I haven't even introduced myself yet. Sorry. I am Leyla, and I'm not usually so ditzy, honest. Oh say you forgive me!"

Lara looked at the girl properly as she put her things back in her bag. Staring back at her with big brown earnest eyes was the girl who had smiled at her... Lara smiled at her warmly. "Don't worry about it, it's my first day too so I know how you feel. My name is Larissa but everyone calls me Lara."

The girl grabbed her hand and shook it enthusiastically. "Great to meet you, now at least I know one person here!"

The two girls went inside and looked around the entrance hall in awe. "Wow," Leyla whispered, "it's like a palace in here!"

Lara nodded mutely. She had never been inside before; it was all that she had imagined and more. Rows of sparkling statues stood at attention under the delicate myriad of arches which interconnected the different areas of the building. The ceiling was so high up it seemed to extend all the way into the sky. She let out a breath she hadn't even realised she was holding. This was all so new to her, and yet she felt a sense of familiarity, of coming home. She looked around the main hall, dozens of equally star struck kids were milling around the statues.

"The key… the time is now… you must save us all…"

Lara looked around to see who had spoken. There was no one standing near her except Leyla. She was staring at Lara with a strange look on her face.

"That wasn't you I heard was it?" she asked Lara.

Lara shook her head. "No, but I hear it too… where did that voice come from?"

Leyla shrugged, "No clue. What do you think it meant?"

"I don't know. I don't even know if whoever it was, was talking to us…"

Lara was interrupted by a loud bang as a huge door at the other end of the hall swung open. A tall woman with long brown hair and twinkling eyes swept through the arch, her dark blue robes fluttering as if she were walking on air.

"Aunt Aelwen," Leyla whispered under her breath.

Lara turned to look at her in surprise. "You know Aunt Aelwen?"

Leyla's cheeks turned pink. "Oops, I was supposed to only call her Miss Ville at school."

"Me too," Lara smiled. "I don't suppose the other kids will like it if they realise we know her from before."

Leyla nodded emphatically. "That's what my dad said too. He's great friends with Aunt Aelwen."

"So is Yelena my foster mother!" Lara exclaimed. "I wonder if your parents know Yelena?"

"Ladies and gentlemen," Aelwen's voice resonated across the stone hall, "permit me to start off the school year by welcoming you all to the Lantis School of Magic. As you may have heard from your parents or older siblings there are many rules to follow. I will inform you of those in due time. Right now, I would like you all to find your rooms and settle in. Get to know your roommates and have a wander round the school. Tomorrow morning we will begin the testing and your class schedule will be drawn up based on your results. Your room numbers are on the scroll hanging on the wall to my left and should you need any help finding your rooms please ask one of the older students who are kindly here today to help you acclimatise."

There was a sudden mad rush towards the scrolls as the students tried to see who they had been paired up with and what room they had gotten. Lara and Leyla hung back until the crowd had thinned before making their way to the wall.

"Yay!!" Leyla squealed. "We're roommates!! I was hoping we would be!!"

"That's brilliant!" Lara beamed. "Let's go find our room! It says we have the River room, which is on the third floor."

They grabbed their bags and raced up the stairs. Once they found their dorm and opened the door they both stopped short in shock. Like everything else at the school, the room was extraordinary. Deep purple curtains framed the large windows and an enormous magenta sofa sat in front of the fireplace. The dark wood floor gleamed and there were two beautiful antique desks on either side of the room surrounded by bookcases filled with books. The main sitting room had two doors, which lead to the girls' own private bedrooms and bathrooms. The bedrooms had been done up in the same plush style and colours as the living room with large canopy beds. And the bathrooms each had their own showers and huge bathtubs with various shades of purple and lilac mosaics on the walls and floors.

"Wow!" Lara gasped as she looked around. "When Yelena told me I was going to be in a dorm this is not what I pictured!"

"Tell me about it," Leyla sighed in wonder. "I may never want to leave this place! It's like something out of a medieval fairy tale!" She jumped on the bed and closed her eyes. "Mmmmm, comfortable too!! I'm definitely going to need that alarm charm my mum made me, or I might never wake up for any of my classes!"

Their suitcases had been brought up while they were in the main hall, and the girls chatted whilst they put their things away, getting to know each other better. They found they had a lot in common. They both loved reading and learning, and came from the same part of Lantis, Karan, one of the nicest areas in the city.

"I'm surprised we never met before," Lara mused. "You live just down the road from me and both of our families know Aunt Aelwen really well. I really have to ask Yelena if she knows your mum and dad."

There was a knock at the door. Leyla jumped off the sofa and yanked the door open. Aelwen was standing there smiling with a bag in her hand.

"Hello girls, I see you've met and had time to settle in."

"Aunt Aelwen!" Lara stood up to give her a hug. "What are you doing here? I thought we weren't supposed to 'know' each other when at school."

She patted Lara's head fondly. "Everyone is too busy at the moment to take any notice of me. Besides, I'm an Elder, do you really think I wouldn't manage to sneak up here unseen?"

"What's in the bag Aunt Aelwen?" Leyla asked excitedly.

"Oh, you girls didn't think that I would let you start magic school and not come by and say hello... or that I wouldn't bring you a small present to mark this special day?"

Leyla jumped up and down excitedly and even Lara, who was desperately trying to seem grown up, was edging closer to Aelwen to peek inside the bag. Aelwen finally took pity on them and took out two velvety soft boxes. Inside each box lay a beautiful silver necklace. Both pendants were carved in silver and they were almost identical except that Lara's had a fiery sun etched on it whilst Leyla's had a crescent moon.

"Wow, Aunt Aelwen, they're amazing!" Lara said happily. "I've never seen anything like it before."

"Yes, thanks so much Aunt Aelwen! It's the best present ever!" Leyla threw her arms around her.

"You're welcome girls," Aelwen replied. "But I need you to make me a promise."

Both girls nodded solemnly at her suddenly serious tone.

"I need you to promise that you will put the necklaces on and not take them off, at least not while you're at school. They have a protection charm built into them and I promised both your parents that I would make sure you were safe. The necklaces will ensure that you are even when I am not around to keep an eye on you."

"Sure," Lara promised. "But we are at magic school. Between the teachers and the elders this must be the safest place on the planets isn't it?"

"I wouldn't have taken mine off anyway!" Leyla twirled round. "It is gorgeous!"

Aelwen nodded. "It is, but it is also a place where you are away from your families for the first time, and left to your own devices for the first time too. Here at school you will find that you are treated very much like an adult. No one will remind you to study; no one will tell you what to do outside of the classroom. You will be completely responsible for yourselves. It sounds great, but it is quite a change from what you are used to as well. Also you know that magic can be dangerous at times, especially in the hands of young students who are new to its subtleties... I just thought that since I was getting you a present anyway I'd help your parents sleep better at night by adding some protection.

"I'm also here for another purpose," Aelwen cleared her throat. "The other Elders will arrive early tomorrow morning and normally we would wait until everyone is on site before we begin testing. However, this year there is an unusually high number of entry level students and we may not finish the testing on time tomorrow. This could be quite inconvenient for us Elders as we are due to go to Rahan the day after to administer the testing at the School of Magic there, then onto Jalyia, Chazma... so if we start running behind it knocks everyone's schedules back. I was wondering if you two wouldn't mind if we tested you today? You only need one Elder present anyway at each testing so it wouldn't be a problem in any way."

"That would be great actually!" Lara said, eyes shining with excitement. "I don't think I would have been able to sleep all night waiting for tomorrow! Will I get the results today?"

"Yes, of course. We wouldn't be so evil as to make you wait a whole day for your results," Aelwen joked.

"Great, let's go then!!" Leyla said, already heading towards the door.

***

The girls followed Aelwen down the long hallway and after what seemed like a million twists and turns through the maze-like building they finally came to a stop in front of a door. They walked into what was obviously some sort of waiting room. There were a couple of sofas pushed up against the walls, a large shiny metal coffee table and a couple of chairs. The room as plush as everything else at the school but sparsely furnished nonetheless. The girls looked around, confused. Was this where they were going to be tested? Aelwen strode in front of them and walked up to a narrow panel on the wall. She then waved her hand across it in a series of symbols. The dark wood panel seemed to glimmer for a moment before vanishing into thin air. In its place appeared an arched entrance way. Aelwen led them through the narrow opening down a long corridor. They came to a cavernous circular chamber. It was a dark room with a lower part which had a pentagram etched in the centre and a raised upper circle surrounding the lower level lined with crimson Varian velvet covered benches. Tall candelabras encircled the stones around the pentagram, the lit candles billowing a sweet scent into the heavy air.

Lara looked around, taking in every detail. She rubbed the goose bumps on her arms. It was more than she had ever imagined it would be. Not even in her wildest dreams had she imagined this, it was like something out of a book. The cave walls arched into a sharp point, ice crystals glinting in the light of the candles.

"Aunt Aelwen, this is something else," Leyla whispered in awe.

She smiled at them warmly. "I remember the first time I was brought in here. I had never seen the like. This is where you are going to be tested. All testing is done in this chamber, but you are the first ones to see it amongst the initiates this year. Normally there are at least three Elders present at the testing, but due to the circumstances it will just be me and two senior Councillors until they arrive. Any questions?"

The girls shook their heads.

"Alright then, let's get started. Who is going first? Lara?"

"Sure Aunt Aelwen," Lara said excitedly.

"Leyla, if you follow that door to your left you will come to a small chamber, you can wait there until we are ready for you... these tests are strictly confidential."

Once Leyla had gone, Aelwen turned to Lara. "Well, there is nothing to be nervous about, this isn't a school test like you are used to, we are not evaluating what you have learnt, only what you are. This will measure your natural magical talents, nothing more. All you have to do is open up to it. Now, you stand here in the centre of the pentagram and I will be observing you from the upper circle with the two councillors," she pointed at a larger bench where a fae and a wizard were taking their seats. "These are Melia and Goran. They will be observing the testing with me."

Lara nodded to the councillors who smiled at her encouragingly. She walked up to the pentagram and took her place. The few seconds it took Aelwen to reach her seat seemed to last an eternity.

"For the official record," Aelwen began, her voice carrying across the massive chamber, "Initiate Lara, age twelve years, resident of Lantis, will commence her test. Witness instructors are Aelwen, Council Elder."

"Melia, Senior councillor," said the fae in her soft voice.

"And Goran, Senior councillor," echoed the wizard.

A scroll appeared out of nowhere, and a quill shot out and starting scribbling furiously on the parchment. Aelwen waited for the pen to finish its records.

"Now then, we are ready to begin." She clapped once and the candles surrounding Lara dimmed until she could no longer see the observers.

A pedestal rose up out of the stone floor in front of Lara. A large purple egg-shaped crystal was perched in a claw setting on top of it.

"Reach out and place both your hands on the crystal Initiate Lara," Aelwen's voice called through the darkness.

Lara did as she was instructed. Contrarily to what she expected, the crystal was warm to the touch and once her hands were in place it seemed to pulsate. Tendrils of light slid out of the crystal, slithering up her hands all the way around her body. Suddenly, Lara felt a pulling sensation and then she was no longer in the testing chamber. She looked around, disorientated at first.

She was in a bright meadow with tall orange grass swaying in the breeze. A silver stream gurgled a few paces away, glinting in the light of the blue sun. Where was she? The sun on the world of Azmantium was red, not blue. And she had never seen orange grass before either.

"Hello young one," a gentle voice startled her. *"Do not fear me. I am part of your 'test' as they like to call it."*

She looked up at the owner of the voice. The stranger had flame red hair speckled with silver strands and kind green eyes.

"Hello," she answered.

"You must be wondering who I am," the lady said. *"Allow me to introduce myself, my name is Caliana. I will be your guide during this test."*

Lara nodded and smiled, and then gasped in surprise as she noticed something truly strange. The lady flickered and Lara could swear that dark green wings erupted out of her back alongside a ridged tail, but a second later they were gone again.

"You're a dragon!" she exclaimed. *"But no one has seen a dragon for years!! I thought you didn't exist anymore!"*

Dragons were the most magical of beings, and contrary to what many people thought, they were actually people who could shape shift into dragons and not mindless savage animals. The Azmantians had once all worshipped dragons but now they were taboo. Lara did not know what had happened, or what the Dragons could have done but even the mention of them was forbidden now. In fact, she only even knew about them from an ancient book she had once found in Yelena's attic.

Caliana's eyes twinkled in merriment. "Interesting—you see me in my true form... but you cannot tell anyone what you see here today, it would be dangerous for all those around you. And I am no more real here than this place the crystal has brought you. Interesting though that you saw that, very interesting..."

Lara fought her disappointment at this news. She had always believed that the dragons were not extinct like people said and that they would return one day. Yelena often told her stories about the Dragons and Lara did not believe that she would do so if the Dragons were evil as the King would have everyone believe. Yelena always described them as powerful but humble and noble people. Caliana smiled at her knowingly and Lara had the strange sensation that she could read her mind.

"Are you ready to begin? Good, then follow me," Caliana swept past her and turned to walk towards the stream.

Lara came to stand next to her by the silver stream and looked at her expectantly. "What exactly do I need to do? They didn't really tell me anything about the test."

Caliana smiled, "The test has already begun my child. This place is as you have imagined it, I too am of your imagination. Everything here is created by your own magic. Each of you will have a different testing experience, their magic will create their own place and guide." She gestured towards the stream. "For the next step you need to step into the stream, close your eyes and open your mind. Just relax and try to blank your mind. Each initiate will be shown something that they need to see… think of it as your magic bonding with you, it has always been inside you but kept apart. Now you need to find it and let it become one with you… don't look so apprehensive, just let it happen."

Lara moved towards the water, marvelling at the iridescent ripples gathering around her ankles. She closed her eyes and let out a deep breath. Her body jolted as images started flashing in her mind in rapid succession.

Two figures stood facing each other, one in a white robe the other in black. They were chanting, their heads bent together, clasping each other's hands. A white light shot up from their hands… then the image changed… there was a man, a young man with long dark hair in purple robes. He stood on a hilltop watching the sunset, she couldn't see his face or make much out, but he was tall and was holding what looked like a small pouch. A hooded woman came up behind him and put her hand on his shoulder, as if comforting him. He shook his head angrily and took something out of the pouch and laid it on the ground. The hilltop was suddenly ablaze, and yet the two figures just stood there unscathed by the dancing flames.

The image changed again and suddenly Lara saw an old woman sitting in a dark cave stirring a boiling cauldron. She was talking to herself worriedly as she watched the potion brew. Smoke spiralled out of the cauldron and formed a crescent moon and a sun, she watched as they gravitated towards each other and then merged. The old lady's eyes turned silver, "You must heed the call; find the answer... burn the darkness with the light... Shadow and light must become one..."

Lara's mind suddenly went blank and she heard Caliana as if from a distance, "We will meet again young one, may your journey be full of light..."

Lara opened her eyes feeling mentally exhausted. She was no longer in the stream but back in the testing chamber. The crystal was dull and colourless now. She stepped back and looked up at the councillors. Melia and Goran were whispering animatedly to each other, and Aelwen was looking at her with an inscrutable look on her face. Aelwen cleared her throat and they fell silent. "Well Lara, your first testing is finished. Now if you can go into the small room and ask Leyla to come in that would be most helpful. Also, it is very important for you to know that whatever you experienced today is strictly confidential. Each testing is a personal journey, a rite of passage if you will. I know it might be frustrating but it really is very important."

"Of course, Elder Aelwen," Lara nodded. "When will I know the results of my test?" She asked a little tentatively.

Aelwen smiled warmly. "I will come to find you later tonight once we have deliberated."

"So how did it go?" Leyla asked her excitedly when she went into the small chamber.

Lara tucked her hair behind her ear absentmindedly. "I'm not sure really, it was all a bit confusing actually. I think it went ok but I didn't really understand what it was all about. Oh, they asked you to go on through."

Leyla hopped off her chair and gave her a quick hug. "Well here goes nothing! Wish me luck!"

Lara returned her hug. "Good luck, you'll be fine."

Leyla winked at her and practically skipped out the door. Lara smiled to herself, it was impossible not to like Leyla, her energy and cheeriness was contagious. She sat down on the sofa while she waited. Her mind was still racing with everything she had seen. What did it all mean? She wasn't sure what she had expected from the testing, but it wasn't that. No one ever talked about what happened during the testing, now she knew why; they weren't allowed to... She was startled to hear the door creak and see Leyla slip into the room.

"That was awesome!" she squealed. "I had no idea!"

"Did it go ok?"

"Yeah, it was definitely something else!" Leyla exclaimed. "Come on let's go to our room. Aunt Aelwen said that we should go on up. She's sending our dinner to our room just for tonight so we can rest a bit. She mentioned that the testing can be very draining so we should take time to recover."

"Ok, sounds good."

"Come on let's go," Leyla pulled her along, "I don't know about you but I'm starving!"

CHAPTER 3

Aelwen frowned at the scrolls in front of her. The two councillors watched her anxiously. The grand chamber was still dimly lit, the shadows of the candles dancing against the walls in silence as the tension in the room grew steadily. Melia looked at Goran expectantly and he shrugged back at her in reply. They would wait until she was ready to speak. They knew that something momentous was happening or about to happen at least. They had been preparing for this day for years, as had countless scores of their ancestors before them. They just didn't know exactly what 'this' was. They had watched Aelwen grow increasingly tense with each passing moment of the two tests. It made them somewhat nervous to see this usually unshakeable woman known for her icy calm demeanour react in such a way. Someone that didn't know her well may not have noticed, but they had been Aelwen's colleagues and friends for over thirty years.

Aelwen passed her hand over the table and the two scrolls instantaneously went up in a blaze of flames. Melia gasped, "Aelwen, what are you doing?" she said trying to salvage what she could of the parchments.

"Leave them be," Aelwen stated calmly.

"But the registrations of the girls…" spluttered Goran at a loss for words.

Aelwen sighed. "There was no other way. No one can know about these two tests, no one can know the results."

"But, destroying the results… that's a crime…" Melia shuddered at the thought.

"Yes," Aelwen acknowledged, "it is a crime punishable by banishment to the Dungeons of darkness, I know… but the Council of Elders cannot be privy to these results. No one can find out about this. It will put in jeopardy everything we have been working for all this time… we cannot let that happen."

"How are we going to get around this problem?" Goran asked. "The council will demand to know why these two haven't been tested, you know that."

Aelwen looked from one to the other. "My friends, I have a great favour to ask both of you. If you feel you cannot do it I will understand. I can perform the mind-wipe so that you won't remember any of this and will be in no danger of being found complicit should anything go wrong… I need you to help me create different results for the tests."

The ensuing silence was deafening. No one spoke for what seemed an eternity as they considered just what they would be agreeing to. Goran was the first to speak, "I will do it," he said calmly. "You are right. I don't know exactly what you saw during the tests, I glimpsed merely a fraction of it, but if you feel that strongly about this, well, I trust your judgement."

Melia nodded. "As do I Elder Aelwen. You have never been one for rash actions, and I have always known you to be wise. I will help you also."

"Thank you my friends, I wish there were another way... I will create the new results and ask that you sign them as witnesses. We shall need to be careful though and to keep a watchful eye on Lara's progress... if she were to exhibit the amount of power in class that I believe she is capable of she would be viewed with suspicion... or worse. We cannot let the Dark Ones find out about them, they are not yet ready. I do not want the King to take note of her in any way. Nor Leyla for that matter... she must also be protected."

"I will ensure that their instructors are sympathetic to our cause, Elder," Goran stated.

"I am already in charge of their dorm wing," Melia said. "I will watch over them as best I can."

They bowed in front of Aelwen and took their leave. Once alone, Aelwen sighed deeply and set to work drawing up the supposed results of the girls.

Lara and Leyla were finishing their dinner when Aelwen knocked on their door. She handed the sealed envelopes into their outstretched hands.

"Let's open them together!" Leyla danced around the room.

They quickly tore open the seals.

"What does yours say? Mine says I am an earth elemental!" Leyla practically shouted gleefully. "I get to do earth magicks!!"

"I am a healer," Lara said. She was a little disappointed that she wasn't an earth elemental like Yelena but she was happy that her power meant she would be able to help people.

"Congratulations girls," Aelwen beamed at them, "those are both very good powers to have, lots of career options."

Healers were in great demand. How sought after they were depended on how strong their healing magic was. And earth elementals could control nature like animals and plants, the strongest elementals could even make things grow out of nothing in the earth. These were great powers to have, but not so rare that anyone would look too closely at the girls, at least that was what Aelwen was counting on. She had destroyed the original results as she didn't want anyone to find out that amazingly Lara had more than one magical power. The Council of Elders would have a fit if they found out that there was every possibility that this child had more magical power in her little toes than the whole of the Elders put together. They would believe the girls to be a danger to society, fearing what they couldn't control… and the King? She couldn't even bear thinking about what he would do if he found out… but Lantis needed Lara. The alternative was unthinkable. Come what may she needed to be protected at all costs. After staying a while to talk with the girls and answer their questions about the school and what they could expect to learn, Aelwen bade them goodnight and left for her own quarters. There was much to be done on this night before she too could seek her bed. She closed the heavy door to her private chambers and did a quick search for magical listening devices. She had yet to find a bug in her room, but she had been taught well to never underestimate the Dark Ones, as she called the King's secret police force charged with seeking out 'traitors' to the throne. Traitors indeed… anyone that disagreed with him and his way of thinking was condemned as a traitor to the Dungeons of Darkness. She waved her hand over a small screen in her office and nodded to the familiar faces that appeared on the other side.

"Good evening, Yelena, Lily. Is Kieran there?"

"We are all here," Kieran, Leyla's father, answered.

Aelwen nodded. "Well then, let's begin… there is much to be done tonight… it is as we thought…"

***

The next morning, Lara was woken up by Leyla jumping on her bed. "Wake up sleepyhead!!" she said, tickling Lara.

"Mmmmm, it's not time to wake up yet," Lara turned her back and hid her head under the covers.

"It's past eight o'clock!! Come on we have to get up!" Leyla yanked the blanket off her impatiently.

"Eight o'clock?! It's still practically night time," Lara yawned. "Besides didn't Aelwen say that we had today off since everyone will be too busy being tested?"

"Exactly! Which means it's the perfect chance to explore the school!! I am dying to see the hidden passageways my mum told me about, I wonder if we'll be able to find them." Leyla's mother, Lily, had also mentioned that no one that she knew had ever found the legendary tunnels, more than likely it was just a story told to young witches and wizards. "Come on Lara, pleeeaase?"

Lara smiled, it was impossible to be annoyed with Leyla for long, especially when she pulled that sweet face. "Ok, ok. Just give me a minute to wake up and I'll come with you." She went to the bathroom and had a quick shower. She was barely finished getting dressed when Leyla bounded back into her room.

"Good, you're nearly ready. I thought we were going to be here all day! Let's go to the dining room and have some breakfast first and then we can start our search."

They found the dining room quite easily despite the labyrinth of corridors and archways to navigate and joined the queue. The room was packed. There were witches, fae and shifters of all ages. Some were joking about with their friends, others practising their magic while they ate. The food smelled delicious.

"Wow! Look at all that food," Leyla was eyeing up the cupcake counter. "I didn't expect there to be so much choice!"

"It's great, isn't it?" said the cheerful looking girl in front of them. She had shoulder length blonde hair and a mischievous smile. "Hi! My name is Anna and this is my friend Sofia," she said pointing at a slightly younger girl with brown hair and big green eyes. "I'm thirteen, and she's twelve. This is our first year too."

"Hi Anna, hi Sofia. I'm Lara and this is Leyla. We're also twelve."

"I'm so excited," Anna smiled. "I have been all year to come here. My parents wouldn't let me come until I turned thirteen though!"

"We are sharing a dorm. Are you two sharing a dorm with each other?" Lara asked.

"Yes," Sofia smiled happily. "We have been friends since we were little. That was one of our parents' conditions actually: they didn't really want us staying with people we didn't know. It's not like my mother isn't going to be hovering about anyway, she works here."

"Is she one of the teachers?" Leyla asked.

"Well, she does teach too, but she is one of the senior councillors based at the school. Her name is Melia."

"Oh, we know her, we met her yesterday. She seemed really nice!" Leyla enthused.

"Yeah, mum's great... but it would be nice if she weren't teaching at school," Sofia said.

"Yeah, how are we supposed to get up to no good with her watching our every move!" laughed Anna. "She's practically my mom too!"

Lara got the impression that they managed it just fine!

Once they had all filled their trays, they headed to a small table towards the back to eat their breakfast. They all laughed when Anna's stomach grumbled loudly.

"What?" she said sheepishly, "I'm hungry. Dinner was eons ago!" And with that she bit into a chunk of cheese and sighed happily. "Mmmmm, this cheese is out of this world," she mumbled between bites. Everyone tried their food, it really was delicious.

"So, what are you guys up to later?" Leyla asked.

"We're going to look for the secret tunnels." Anna waved her fork around enthusiastically, almost poking Sofia in the eye. "Oops, sorry!"

Sofia smiled. "We can help you look! We've been to the school so many times to see my mum that we know every corner of it!"

"Great!" The two girls beamed at each other. Leyla's face dropped. "But don't you need to get tested?"

"Mine is in five minutes, and Sofia is just after me... if you don't mind waiting a little bit we can all go together. When is your testing?"

"We had ours last night," Lara explained. "There were too many applicants to get through in one day so we were tested early."

"Cool!" Anna was obviously dying to ask what their talent was but she kept quiet. She got up, followed by her friend. "How about we meet you in the main entrance hall then, in about twenty minutes?"

"Great, good luck both of you."

"See you in a bit," Leyla waved.

***

"Gods above!" Anna shouted as she ran towards them in the hall causing people to look at her. "I'm a protector!! How cool is that!!! And Sofia is an illusionist!" She hugged Lara and then Leyla.

"Congratulations, that's wonderful," Lara said to both of them.

"So what are you guys?" Sofia asked curiously. "If you don't mind telling us that is," she added as an afterthought.

Lara laughed. "That's ok, it's not a secret or anything, I'm a healer and Leyla is an elemental."

"Cool," Sofia looked at Leyla in awe. "I've never met an elemental. You're going to have so much fun in class!! Mum told me that elementals get to do most of their classes outside so they can practice with nature! Although from what I've heard all the classes here are fun, not like the other schools we've been to... here it's all about magic! Come on, I'll show you where the classrooms are!"

They walked off arm in arm with Lara and Leyla following them.

"Healing magic is one of the strongest talents there is. You're so lucky... although I've heard that some of the stuff you have to learn is pretty gruesome, and you'll have to be dealing with sick people for practice," Leyla shuddered. "Sorry, I'm a bit squeamish, just as well I'm not a healer, it wouldn't exactly give the patients confidence if I passed out while treating them!"

"I don't mind all that," Lara said. "I think I'll enjoy helping people."

They walked into a large hexagonal chamber. It looked like an auditorium with its raised levels of benches wrapped all around the room.

"This is the healers' chamber," Sofia announced.

Lara stared in awe at the impressive room. There was a bed in the centre of the room, probably where the patients would lie while being treated. She imagined herself sitting on one of the benches in the viewing gallery as she watched an expert healer at work. She couldn't wait to start. The arched ceiling was covered in healing books, but she couldn't see any ladders to get to them.

"Ah, trying to figure it out are you?" a silver-haired old wizard said kindly from behind her. "It gets them every time!" he chuckled.

"Hello Healer Thomas," Anna greeted him.

"Well, good morning Anna, Sofia… and who might your young friends be?"

"This is Lara and Leyla," Sofia exclaimed. "And Lara is a healer like you!"

"Ah, another healer, very good—there are not enough healers to go around. I will be one of your teachers then." He winked. "So would you like to know how to get the books down from up there?"

Lara nodded earnestly.

"Well, I am a hard task master, and I like my students to do their work. It is a waste of time if you come to class unprepared, so I created a system where only students who know what book they need can get to it. Once you know the title of the book you need all you have to do is call it down. Observe; *Magical mysteries of medicine*," he called out loudly. A big brown leather clad book floated down from the ceiling into his hands. "So you see," he said, eyes twinkling. "If you want to have the help of my books in your studies you must do your homework. And now if you don't mind ladies, I need to start preparing my classroom for tomorrow's lesson."

They said goodbye and continued their exploration of the school. They looked into countless classrooms, walked under numerous grand arches... they looked into every nook and cranny, but they didn't find any signs of hidden passageways.

"I'm tired," Sofia moaned at last, "and hungry. I can't believe we missed lunch and we didn't even find any tunnels."

Anna looked thoughtful. "I wonder... what if they are hidden?"

"We already know they are hidden," Sofia rolled her eyes.

"No," Anna said. "I mean what if they are hidden by magic?

"That makes perfect sense!" Lara exclaimed. "What would be the point of hiding a tunnel in magic school without magic?"

"But how will we find it if it's hidden by magic?" Leyla asked.

"Yeah. None of us knows how to do any of that yet!" Sofia agreed.

"There's no rush. We will find it eventually. I can feel it. Once we learn more of our magic, and maybe with a little research in the magic library... we will find it if it exists."

"Lara is right," Anna said. "We can even ask mum which books may help us find a spell to unlock the tunnels' magic. But for now, let's go and grab some food before we miss dinner too!"

CHAPTER 4

The dining hall was awash with excited chatter as everyone talked about what talent they had and who was in whose class. The girls got their food and sat down at a long table in the middle of the hall. They had just started eating when an older girl plonked her tray on their table.

"Well, well, what do we have here?" she sneered.

The girls looked up, the girl was expensively dressed and her hair was done up in the latest Rahanian fashion.

"Hello," Lara said to her.

"Oh, it speaks!" the girl cackled. "Guys you have to come here and see this!"

Two more girls and three boys joined her.

"Look at these pathetic sad initiates... they look lost don't you all think? I mean why else would they be sitting at our table? Obviously they aren't clever enough to have figured out that no one sits here but us. Now they have gone and contaminated our table with their disgusting auras."

Silence cut through the entire dining hall as everyone quietened and stared at them.

"Since it's your first day I think I'll go easy on you," she continued. Then she waved her hand over a glass of water and it poured down Anna's head. The whole room held its breath. Lara looked at Anna's usually smiling face. There were unshed tears in her eyes and her lips were trembling. Something snapped inside of Lara. Before she had time to think about it she had stood up and with a flick of her wrist she had the girl suspended in the air. The girl was staring at her in shock. Then Lara flicked her wrist again and all the glasses of water from the tables around them came whizzing by to dump themselves on her. The other students in the hall starting laughing and clapping as they watched the school's resident mean girl being given a taste of her own medicine, hanging there in the air, painstakingly done up hair now a sodden mess.

The girl screamed, "How dare you!? Put me down now!!"

"That's enough my dear." Aelwen came up from behind Lara, her serious tone belied by the mirth in her eyes. "I'll take it from here."

"I want her expelled! That brat doesn't know who she's messed with! We'll see how she…"

"Quiet!!" Aelwen roared as she glared at her. "You will hold your tongue Jayla, unless you also want to be expelled for picking on initiates?"

"But I didn't, they…"

"I said quiet." The icy chill in her voice stopped Jayla's rant. "I witnessed the whole thing. And what I saw was a table of initiates happily enjoying their first day until a senior student decided to ruin it for them. Lara did nothing more than she should have, she was acting out of kindness to a friend, you would do well to learn from her."

"Wait until my father hears of this!" Jayla said menacingly.

"I think you forget that I too am an Elder, and that I am the headmaster here not your father. But since you will not apologize nor see reason, I have no choice but to punish you. You will help clean the school for a month and your outing privileges are revoked until otherwise stated." Aelwen spun on her heel and walked off, leaving behind an enraged Jayla. She glared at the four girls before stomping off out of the hall.

"I'm sorry about that," one of the boys in Jayla's group said, staring at Lara. "I'm Xan, Jayla shouldn't have done what she did."

Lara looked at him, slightly disconcerted by his staring at her and still angry over what had been done to Anna. "Well, if you were really sorry you would have stopped her or intervened at least. You just stood there." She looked at the other four in his group. "None of you did anything at all. Whatever you have to do or say please go elsewhere so we can go back to enjoying ourselves." With that she sat back down, turned her back on Xan and continued eating.

Xan went to sit at another table with his friends. He couldn't help staring at this girl, Lara. She was absolutely stunning, long glossy chestnut hair and the most beautiful blue eyes framed with pitch black lashes.

"Stop drooling," his friend Andrew elbowed him in the ribs, "you've got no hope in hell with that one... even if she survives Jayla and your brothers."

"Yeah," Meredith said. "No way Jayla is going to take that lying down! That girl humiliated her in front of the whole school."

"She deserved it," Xan muttered under his breath. He was ashamed by what Lara had said, it was true, he hadn't done anything to stop Jayla in all the years she had bullied everyone around her. It had always seemed easier to just follow in her wake. He had never joined in when Jayla and his brothers picked on anyone, but the look in Lara's eyes really brought it home that doing nothing was just as bad.

"Besides," Meredith added, "there's something off about that girl."

Andrew nodded in agreement. "She only just got here bro, there's no way she should have that kind of power already."

Xan nodded absentmindedly as he watched Lara from the corner of his eye. There was something about her... something different.

Lara hugged Anna when the others left. "Are you ok?" she asked, drying Anna's face with a napkin that one of the other students had kindly gotten her.

"I'm great!" Anna squealed. "That was awesome! How did you do it?"

Lara looked confused.

"Yeah, you totally levitated her!!" Anna chimed. "She so deserved it, mum has told me all about that family.

She's Elder Jamal's daughter, spoilt little brat! So 'fess up, how did you do it?"

Lara shrugged. "I really don't know. I just remember getting so angry; I wasn't even thinking... it just happened."

"Well, it was awesome," Leyla said hugging her.

Lara was glad to see Anna back to her normal self.

"Don't look now but that boy is still staring at you," Leyla whispered. "It's kind of creepy."

"Well as long as he and his 'friends' leave us alone then I really couldn't care what he's doing. Although, I wouldn't be surprised if Jayla tried something... I think we should all be careful around her."

"Don't worry," Sofia said. "We will be, and I'm sure Aelwen will be watching her too, as well as my mum. My mum can't stand Jayla, she said Jayla was a bad influence and warned us not to hang out with her, as if we would!"

Later that evening Anna and Sofia had gone off to their own dorm, and Leyla had already gone to bed. Lara was reading one of the medical magic books that had appeared on her bookshelf when there was a gentle knock at the door. She opened the door softly and saw Aelwen waiting on the other side.

"Come in," she told her.

Aelwen walked in and sat on the sofa. "I am surprised to see you still up, although it's just as well you're a night owl like me because I needed to talk to you."

"Am I in trouble Aunt Aelwen?"

She chuckled quietly, "No my dear, not at all. I daresay we've all been waiting a long time for someone to put Jayla in her place. You have nothing to be sorry about. But I did want to ask you how you were able to do what you did. That was some pretty powerful magic you demonstrated for an initiate."

"I really don't know. I thought about it, but I've never done anything like that before, and I honestly don't know how it happened. Was it not supposed to happen, is something wrong with my magic?"

"Not at all," she reassured her. "Magic is a part of us—it's in our very essence. You just happen to have stronger magic than expected, so when you got angry I suspect the magic tied to your emotions got amplified."

"Ok, thanks for explaining it to me," Lara smiled, relieved.

"You're welcome my dear. But I do have to warn you that it would be best if you tried to control your emotions while you are at school. You haven't had any magical instruction yet and it would be very easy for your control to slip... it might attract some unwanted attention. Just bear that in mind. Yes?" she asked seriously.

"Of course. But whose attention would I be attracting?"

"Well, magic school is an extremely safe place. It should be, I designed the wards on it," she joked. "But there are undesirables in all places in the world. There are people looking to take advantage of those with a lot of natural power. I just don't want you to fall in with the wrong people."

Lara nodded, Yelena was always telling her the same thing.

Aelwen stood up. "Now then, I should leave you to get to bed. You will need your rest tonight because tomorrow you start your first lessons. I believe your first class is with Healer Thomas?"

"Yes, after that I have History of Magic, Herbology and Spells. Potions is not until the next day."

"Ah yes, Potions, always one of my favourite classes… which is why I am teaching it this year."

Lara looked surprised. "I thought you only gave occasional classes?"

"The Elders thought it would be too much for my work load with all the other things requiring my attention, but I finally convinced them of the benefits to having an Elder teach full time," her eyes twinkled. "And that said—I really must go. Goodnight dear child." She brushed a kiss on Lara's forehead.

"Good night Aunt Aelwen," Lara yawned.

The next morning the girls walked to their classes. Apart from the classes for their own individual talents all of the other classes were compulsory for everyone so they would be together after their first sessions. Lara hurried to Healer Thomas's classroom. She felt a bit groggy having not gone to bed 'til late. There were three other students in the chamber. She was annoyed to see that one of them was Xan. He was wearing the darker robes of an assistant Healer—great, so she would have to put up with him all year. She sat as far away from him as possible. Healer

Thomas appeared in the middle of the room in a flash of light, startling them all.

"Good morning," he said cheerfully. "Don't mind me, I like to make an entrance."

Lara found herself smiling, all trace of nerves wiped away. She sat through the whole class paying attention to everything the teacher said and taking notes. It was all fascinating, and Healer Thomas was a captivating teacher. She could hardly believe it when a loud gong sounded, signalling the end of the lesson.

"Well, that's it for today. I'll be seeing you all again tomorrow at the same time. I want you all to find out the best method for dispelling a malicious hex. And if you do a good job I'll see about bringing in one of my patients for an observation session." With that he vanished into thin air.

Lara was almost out of the door when Xan caught her arm. "Lara, hi. Look I really am sorry about yesterday. I know you're upset but we're in the same classes. Do you think we could just start over?"

Lara paused and looked at the tall boy with the kind brown eyes standing in front of her so earnestly. "Fine. But that does not include making friends with Jayla." She swept through the door to her next class.

He hurried after Lara as she strode to her next class in the hopes of sitting next to her. He wanted to talk to her some more but by the time he got there Lara was already sitting at a table with her three friends.

"You done staring at the losers' table?" Jayla crept up behind him and sneered in his ear. "I wouldn't get too attached to them," she continued. "I have a feeling they won't be here much longer."

"Jayla, what are you up to now?"

"Oh nothing... but you never know when something bad will happen, all these initiates with so little control over their magic... well anything can happen." She levelled a glare at the girls' table and sashayed towards another table where her friends were waiting for her. Xan followed her and sat down. He peered at Lara again. She was completely oblivious to him and Jayla, lost in conversation with her friends. He couldn't figure her out. He was the King's son, everyone wanted to be his friend... she was different though, she didn't seem to care about his status at all. He watched as Max, one of the senior wizards sat down next to her and she laughed at something he said. Jayla leaned over towards him.

"Oooh, trouble in paradise? I don't think that loser is interested in you Xan. And Max is dreamy... tall, handsome, and did I mention his gorgeous green eyes? Maybe he's asking her out, she definitely looks interested."

"Shut up Jayla, you don't know what you're talking about."

"Really?" she practically purred. "That's not what I heard. A little birdie told me that you've been trying to talk to her," she scowled at him menacingly. "You'd better not go there Xan, because we're practically family and family sticks together... that girl is going to get what she deserves as is anyone on her side."

"You are not my family," he replied.

Jayla shrugged. "Maybe not yet, but everyone knows that Seth and I will be married one day—and when that happens not only will I be your sister but I will be queen." She glanced at him, a calculating look in her eyes. "So maybe you should watch how you treat me. After all you are only the third son... the least important of the heirs," she quipped with a toss of her head.

CHAPTER 5

The days went by quickly as the girls went to classes. They had both settled in well and made lots of new friends. Most of the other students were really friendly and nice, and there hadn't been any more trouble from Jayla and her gang so far. They just avoided each other if their paths crossed. Lara and Leyla had become very close to Anna and Sofia, and most evenings they would hang out together in their room, doing homework and chatting. On the weekends they all went home to see their parents. Since it had turned out that Yelena knew Leyla's parents already and the girls got along so well, they had all started meeting up for Sunday lunch. Lara really liked Leyla's parents and felt completely at home in their house too. Leyla's mother, Lily, was just as chatty and friendly as Leyla and although her father Kieran was a quiet man, he too was kind and always had a twinkle in his eyes. She had already gotten to know Anna's mum Melia at school, and had found her to be really caring and bubbly, always happy to stop for a chat. Sofia's mother and father, Sarra and Daniel, were best friends with Melia and Xor, Anna's father. All their parents worked for the Council in some capacity, but Melia was the only one that taught at the school. Lara had gotten to know her particularly well as she was her assigned mentor as well as teaching her herbology class. She was a fantastic teacher for those who wanted to learn; enthusiastic, informed... she kept all of the classes fun and her students all loved her.

"The Elders are coming to examine the magic registrations this week," Lily announced at Sunday lunch one week.

"Really?" Leyla asked. "That's great! I've been waiting to meet them all for ages!"

Neither of the girls noticed the glance that passed between Lily and Yelena.

"Well, I don't know if you're going to actually meet them," Lily's smile didn't reach her eyes. "I think they are going to lead an assembly, but aside from that they don't usually stick around for long."

"I want to see what Akkarin's like!" Leyla said in awe. "He is the most powerful wizard in the worlds!! Apart from the King of course," she amended hurriedly.

Lily laughed. "You should have seen her room a few years ago! It was covered in posters of Akkarin... I think she single-handedly kept his fan club going!"

Leyla flushed a deep shade of red.

Lily chuckled. "I think she still has that little figurine of him in her bedside cabinet."

"Hey!" Leyla grumbled good-naturedly. "It's a collector's item! I couldn't just get rid of it."

Everyone laughed as Leyla continued to grumble under her breath.

"Is everything in place?" Yelena asked nervously once the girls had gone out shopping.

Lily nodded. "Aelwen has taken care of it. Both the girls' results have been amended."

Yelena shivered, "I don't want to even think of what will happen if they find out what we've done…"

***

"Is it time to get up already?" Leyla grumbled on Monday morning, "I just went to bed a minute ago!"

Winter had arrived and the sky was dark purple in the mornings, not turning lilac until quite late in the day making it seem like it was night time for longer. Leyla was struggling with the dark days unlike Lara who was always up early reading up on the week's healing lessons.

Lara smiled, "Morning sleepy head!"

"Argh, how are you always so cheerful in the mornings!?" Leyla groaned dramatically. "And you're already showered and dressed!"

"I want to get to class early today, Healer Thomas is going to bring in an actual live patient!" Lara said excitedly. "He said he is going to pick one of us to diagnose and treat her!"

"Cool," Leyla said as she brushed the knots out of her hair. "I might be a while, why don't you head down to breakfast? I will meet you there later."

Lara didn't have to be told twice. She grabbed her books and her bag and darted out of the room. She was in such a hurry that she didn't see the boy in her way until she had collided into him.

"Oh, I'm so sorry!" she exclaimed as she helped him pick his books and hers off the floor. "I wasn't looking where I was going!" She looked up to find Xan smiling at her.

"That's ok," he said with humour. "You were obviously lost in thought. Something to do with the live patient perhaps?"

Lara nodded. "I was hoping to get into class early and prepare."

"Well, I had the same thought... do you want to go to breakfast together? I don't think many people will be there yet as it's so early."

"Sure," she smiled at him as he took her books from her so he could carry them.

The cafeteria was deserted when they got there. Lara grabbed an apple off the platter and took a seat.

"Is that all you're eating?" Xan asked as he sat across from her with a plate heaped with eggs and bacon, a hot chocolate and a huge bowl of cereal.

"I'm too excited to eat," she confessed as she absentmindedly bit into her apple. "I've been waiting weeks for this!"

Xan laughed as he quickly shovelled some eggs into his mouth. "I don't think I've ever seen anyone so excited to meet their first patient before. I'll warn you though, it can be quite gory... one of the girls passed out last year."

"We don't know if it's 'my' patient yet, Healer Thomas hasn't said," Lara shrugged.

Xan arched a brow, "Seriously? Who else is he going to pick? You have been his best student by about a mile...

as well as the only one of us who truly seems destined to become a healer."

"You don't want to be a healer?"

He shrugged, "It's cool being able to help people... I just don't feel that it's what I'm meant to do in the future. I know that probably doesn't make any sense—call it a gut feeling."

"No, I get it. Healing calls me to in a way that potions class doesn't... I guess I just thought that anyone with healing abilities would want to become a healer—there's such a shortage of them."

He nodded in agreement. "That's true, but you have to remember that not everyone with healing abilities has enough magicks to become a truly good healer—my healing magicks are quite weak compared to my illusionist magicks—that's my main area of power."

"So, do you know what you want to do when you finish school?" Lara asked, genuinely interested.

Xan shrugged, "I'm not sure yet... my father wants me to join the royal guard as an illusionist but I don't know if I really want a military career—it's not like anything ever happens on Azmantium. I don't know what the guards do all day long except for training exercises. I guess you want to be a healer?"

Lara nodded as she finished her apple. "Definitely, if I can get the grades for it!" She stood up, "Come on, let's go to the healing chamber, Healer Thomas is probably already there!"

He smiled at her enthusiasm as he put their trays on the cart by the door and followed in her wake.

"Good morning Healer Thomas!" Lara said as she burst into the chamber excitedly.

Healer Thomas looked up from where he was sitting at his desk. He was barely visible behind the piles of books stacked in front of him.

"Why am I not surprised that you are the first one here?" he chuckled. "Well, you might as well help me prepare the room since you are here so early." He stood up and waved his hand. The solid steel door of the large supplies cupboard swung open and a silver hospital bed floated out and over into the middle of the hexagonal chamber. "This is what I need prepared before our patient arrives," he said, handing her a list.

Lara looked at the sheet of paper in her hand. There was a long list of herbs and plants scribbled on it, as well as some rarer items.

"Are all these necessary to cure what the patient has?" she asked confused.

"No my dear," Thomas's eyes twinkled with merriment. "Were our patient to need all of that she would be gravely ill indeed! But since you do not yet know what ails our subject, it is always wisest to work with a full inventory of supplies at hand—you never know when you will need something."

Lara nodded and walked over to the supplies cupboard, although it was more like a small room than a cupboard. She started to look through the various rows of meticulously organised shelves for the herbs.

Healer Thomas turned to Xan. "I believe your early presence has less to do with healing and more to do with a certain young healer," he said amused as Xan flushed slightly. "But, since you are here, why don't you help me set up the spectator's area at the back. A few of the Elders have voiced an interest in observing our diagnosis and treatment class."

Xan nodded and followed his teacher. Thomas showed him how he wanted the room arranged and together they quickly used their magicks to reorganise the seating in the lecture room. Within moments they had set up a row of seating creating a gallery where everyone would have a good view of the bed.

"Thank you young Xan," his teacher said.

"Which Elders are coming?" Xan asked.

"Elders Jamal, Aelwen, Akkarin and Olivia will all be here today. The only one that cannot make it is Elder Michael—he is at a meeting with the King. Speaking of which, how is your father these days Xan? We haven't had the pleasure of his visit in quite some time."

"He is well thank you," Xan replied. "Busy as always though…"

"Of course," Healer Thomas nodded. "Well, look at that—young Lara has already prepared our room for us— and a fine job you have done!" he smiled at her as she put the last flasks on the side tables around the bed. He glanced around the room quickly. "Perfect, it is all ready." He pressed the amethyst on the cuff at his wrist.

"Hello Healer Thomas," a kindly voice came out of the stone.

"Good morning Maribel, would you be kind enough to send in our patient?" he asked the school's receptionist.

"Straightaway Sir," she said before breaking the connection.

CHAPTER 6

There was a knock at the door. A tall thin woman walked in nervously. She was pale and sallow with sunken silver eyes that seemed too large for her face. Her hair was prematurely streaked with grey and her hands were shaking tremulously. There was a deep sadness in her eyes.

"Come in Elina," Healer Thomas said kindly as he gently escorted her to the bed. "It is good to see you again."

The woman called Elina nodded shyly. "Thank you Healer Thomas, it is good to see you too."

"Come and lie down my dear," he said, helping her onto the bed. "These are two of my best students, Lara and Xan."

They smiled at her as her misty eyes settled on them.

"Such pretty hair you have," Elina said wistfully to Lara. "I used to have pretty hair too... but now I am withered and drained."

Lara looked at Healer Thomas, uncertain how to react to this.

"Don't you worry my dear," he said to Elina, "we will have you back to yourself in no time at all. Lara will be the one helping me today. She is a fine healer."

Elina nodded and closed her eyes.

The awkward moment was broken by the arrival of the other students. Lara inspected Elina discreetly while her friends took their seats. Something seemed off about the woman. She looked old and shrivelled and yet... something unnatural seemed to be going on.

Healer Thomas clapped his large hands together twice and silence fell across the chattering students. "Class, this is Elina. She has graciously agreed to be our patient for the day. I assure you that her malady is real and so must the treatment be. I have chosen Lara to help me today but do not worry yourselves—you will all have a turn in time." He waved his hands and dimmed the lights slightly. "Now, I want you all on your very best behaviour as we have some special guests coming today. Elders Jamal, Akkarin, Aelwen and Olivia will be sitting in on our class."

An excited chatter started up at the back of the room. Healer Thomas clapped his hands once more. "Now, I understand how exciting this is for you all... however, I will not tolerate any misbehaviour. This is a real patient and we will treat her as such—I want you all to imagine that we are in a real hospital and that this is your patient. We will treat our patients with respect and consideration at all times."

A loud knock sounded and the door swung open. Elder Aelwen walked in with a woman and two men Lara didn't know. Everyone watched in silence as they made their way to the front of the gallery and took their seats. The tallest man in their group stood up and turned to the class. His long dark hair hung down to his waist, and his black eyes gleamed in the half-light.

"Good morning students, I am Akkarin, Head of the Council of Five. I thank you, as well as Healer Thomas, on behalf of myself and my colleagues for inviting us here today to observe your teaching. Elder Aelwen you all know already," he gestured towards her. "And these are Elders Jamal and Olivia."

Elder Jamal was a nondescript man of medium height and build. There was nothing remarkable about his dark blonde hair or his face except for the watchful manner in which he was looking around the classroom. A strange expression flickered across his face briefly but was quickly replaced by a smile when he was presented to the class. Lara snuck a quick peak at Elder Olivia. She was stunning. Tall and slim with long blonde hair and sparkling blue eyes—she sat gracefully next to Aelwen and smiled warmly at everyone.

"Good morning Elders," Healer Thomas bowed slightly. "It is an honour indeed to have you present today."

Elder Akkarin nodded at him.

"Well," Healer Thomas continued, "you have chosen a fine day to sit in on our class indeed. We will be examining our first patient of the term." He turned to the class and pointed to the bed. "This is Elina. I have chosen our newest student, Lara, to help with the diagnosis and treatment today." He looked at the Elders. "Lara is our youngest student, but she has shown a fine affinity and interest for healing."

Lara tried not to blush as all eyes turned to her. She suddenly felt very small standing in the centre of the chamber with all her fellow students and Elders looking down on her from the viewing gallery. She glanced at Xan sitting in the front row, he smiled at her encouragingly.

"Now, Lara if you will my dear," Healer Thomas stepped aside to allow her to move next to the patient. "The first thing I want you to do is to examine your patient."

Lara gave Elina a small smile as she stood next to the bed.

"May I begin?" she asked Elina.

Elina nodded nervously, seeming younger suddenly.

"There is nothing to be worried about," Lara reassured her. "This is not going to hurt at all, and I will tell you what I am going to do every step of the way. I promise I will do nothing that you don't want and if at any time you are uncomfortable or want me to stop all you have to do is say."

"Okay," Elina said less worriedly this time.

Lara reached her hands over Elina, placing one just a few centimetres away from her forehead and the other hovering over her stomach.

"I am just going to check you over to begin with," Lara said in her sweet reassuring voice. "You will feel a slight warmth as I pass my hands over your body to find the cause of your illness."

Lara closed her eyes and concentrated on directing her magicks to Elina's body. A soft glowing light flowed from her hands and settled over Elina.

"It is warm!" Elina exclaimed.

"Is it uncomfortable?" Lara asked, still with her eyes shut.

"No," Elina shook her head, "it is quite pleasant actually."

Lara passed her hands over Elina's entire body from head to toe. Once she had done so she returned to Elina's head and placed both of her hands on Elina's hair gently. Her eyes flew open as her hands made contact with her patient's body. The chamber disappeared from her sight as she was flooded with a stream of images. She stiffened as Elina's memories poured into her.

A young girl wept as she was pulled forcibly away from her mother. She looked no older than eight years old. She cried out as men in dark cloaks dragged her away. Then another image—the same girl sitting in a small room with only a bed and a chair, all huddled up into a ball as she rocked herself frantically. She looked up suddenly as there was a loud knock at the door and froze in terror.

"You have been summoned; it is time for you to earn your keep," a deep voice said as two men in crimson cloaks walked to the bed and grabbed her roughly by the shoulders.

"I want to go home!" The young girl cried out. "I want my mother!"

"You will do as you are told, or you will never see your mother again!" The deep voice boomed. "You have been granted a great honour today... others would give everything to be in your place you ungrateful child!" With that he turned on his heel and swept away as the girl was half dragged, half carried behind him.

The image faded as another bombarded Lara. *The girl was older now, perhaps around sixteen. She sat listlessly in a dark chamber as a hooded man stood in front of her.*

"*Tell me again!*" *the man roared at her cowering figure.* "*This time speak plainly, I grow weary of your riddles Oracle!*"

"*What I speak, 'tis always true. But you will not hear the truth as you do not know how to listen.*"

"*You dare talk to me in such a manner?!*" *he bellowed in the girl's face.*

"*I dare nothing. I merely speak the words of the Gods—I am but their messenger. And for all your power and finery you are still nothing but a man... I warn you now since you seek the future so impatiently that your time is coming to an end—there is now one more powerful than you with whom you must contend.*"

"*Who is it!?*" *he shouted, shaking her roughly.* "*Tell me who this person is!*"

She shook her head, "*That I cannot do as that knowledge is blocked from me... I grow weak from your constant demands. I have little power left to foresee the future.*"

The man turned angrily towards another man standing in the shadows. "*What is this? I asked you to find me an Oracle... you brought me a pathetic excuse of one. She cannot tell me what I want to know!*"

The other man bowed slightly. "*Master, she was the only one I could find... the others are all in hiding. We only found this one because one of her neighbours saw her using her powers and mentioned it to one of our men.*"

"*This is not good enough!*" *the first man banged his fist on the wooden table in the corner.*

"*I understand Master... but I did warn you that tapping into that amount of power before she came of age would burn her out quickly. We should have waited until she was older before using her—now she hardly has any power left.*"

"*Well, she will remain here and serve me until every last drop of magic is gone from her body... I will have my answers!*" the first man ordered.

The memory that hit Lara next took her breath away. *It was the same girl; although she was no longer a girl but a woman... her once blond hair was grey and brittle, her hands skeletal and frail. She sat in a dark room by herself. She did not even look up at the sound of her door opening—she was past caring now.*

"*Hurry!*" *a voice said to her urgently.* "*If I am to get you out of here, we must hurry!*"

The woman did not even blink; it was as if she couldn't hear the man.

He walked over to the bed and knelt in front of her, clasping her hands. "*Please,*" *he beseeched her,* "*this is the only chance we will have of getting you out of here. There are people waiting for you outside, good people that will help you but we have to go now.*"

"*I have no magic left now,*" *she said calmly.* "*There is nothing more he can do to me.*"

"*Please,*" *he begged,* "*your mother is waiting for you; she has been looking for you all these years!*"

"*My mother is dead,*" *she said flatly.*

"*No!*" *the man said forcefully,* "*she is very much alive and well, they told you that to hurt you, to keep you here.*"

The woman looked up suddenly. Lara recoiled in shock as she saw the woman's eyes—they were silver and worn out. The girl was Elina. She was not an old woman at all. Her youth had been sucked out of her with her magic.

She blinked and removed her hands from her head. Elina was looking at her knowingly. She gestured to Lara. Lara bent down as Elina spoke in her ear. "You must keep what you have seen to yourself... there is great danger in speaking of such things."

Lara nodded numbly, she looked around the room. No one seemed to have noticed anything strange going on.

"Well, my dear, have you reached a diagnosis?" Healer Thomas asked, interrupting her inner musings.

Lara nodded. "This patient has suffered a great trauma which has drained her magicks."

"Very good, Lara," Healer Thomas said. "Do you know of any treatments for such a malady?"

Lara nodded. "Yes Sir, there are a number of different healing potions, spells and methods we can use to try to reignite the magicks." She turned to Elina, "I am sorry there is no quick fix, we can help to an extent. Your health will improve with each treatment but your powers will never be what they were if they even come back at all."

Elina nodded. Lara could swear that she seemed relieved that her powers were gone for good.

"Now Lara, which treatment would you recommend in this particular instance?" Healer Thomas asked.

"I think a mixture of small daily doses of energy healing combined with witchbane tonic would probably work best in this instance."

"And why did you choose this particular method?" Healer Thomas asked in surprise.

Lara looked up at him. "We could subject her to magic fire, it would probably be the quickest way to get her magic back, but the patient's body is weak. I do not know if the cure would be worse than the illness. I believe it is best to go slowly, allowing the body time to readjust."

Silence met her words. She looked at Healer Thomas. He was watching her with a strange expression on his face. Had she said something wrong? She waited nervously, the silence almost deafening now.

"Well," Healer Thomas spoke finally, "I can honestly say that I am astounded Lara." He smiled at her. "There's no need to look so worried dear. The treatment you prescribed is perfect in this instance." He shook his head, "I am merely amazed that you did not choose one of the other methods—most novice healers would seek a method with faster results. You have shown a maturity beyond your years and chosen what is truly best for your patient—something I would expect from an experienced Healer. You truly have a talent for healing my dear."

He turned to the class. "I believe this class has been most educational for you all. I hope you will retain what you have learnt today. Now, I would like to thank Elina for coming in and allowing us to work on her—it is most daunting to be examined in front of such a large audience. And thanks also to Lara."

Elder Akkarin stood. "I would like to thank you Healer Thomas for allowing us to intrude on your lesson— it has been most enlightening." He turned to Lara, "I am most impressed young lady. I hope that you will consider a future career in healing. I will be following your progress with interest."

The other Elders rose and followed him out of the room.

Lara stayed behind to help tidy the chamber once everyone had left except for her, Elina and Healer Thomas.

"Elina, I have a suggestion to make," Thomas said to her. "I think that Lara should be in charge of your treatments if that is agreeable to you. I will be supervising of course. But I truly think it would benefit the both of you."

Elina nodded. "Yes Healer, I would like that also."

"What do you say Lara?" Healer Thomas asked her.

"Wow!" she exclaimed. "That would be great! If you're sure I'm ready for that?"

He nodded. "I believe you have a free period just now?" he asked.

Lara nodded.

"In that case, since there's no time like the present, why don't you stay here and start Elina's first treatment?"

Lara nodded eagerly and looked at Elina.

"Why not?" Elina said.

"Why don't you lie back down?" Lara smoothed the bed sheets. "I will just go prepare the witchbane—it will only take a few minutes. And once you've drunk the potion we can start the energy healing."

Healer Thomas sat next to Elina once Lara had gone into the storeroom to get the ingredients she needed.

"Is this a good idea?" Elina asked him once Lara was out of earshot.

He nodded gravely. "It is imperative that she learns to use her powers sooner rather than later Elina, you have foreseen this much yourself."

Elina smiled sadly. "It is a long and hard path she must walk Healer Thomas. I have felt her essence, she is the brightest light amongst us... I wish there were another way. I wish we could spare her from what is to come."

"As do I Elina," Healer Thomas sighed. "She has a real talent for healing... and were the situation different she would make an excellent Healer. But her destiny calls, and so must she follow."

"Destiny is never set in stone Healer, you know this. Our choices and those of the ones around us will ultimately determine the outcome of our lives. Know this though Healer, if it is ever in my power to protect this child I will do so, destiny or not. Throughout my many years of captivity and the many gruesome things that I was forced to witness for his sake, all that kept me sane were the glimpses of Lara and the hope she instilled in me—I owe much to her."

CHAPTER 7

"The potion is ready Elina," Lara bustled back in with a clear flask filled with a bright orange liquid. "I hope you don't mind but I mixed some elfberries into the bane. It won't be any less effective, but it will definitely taste better!"

Healer Thomas smiled at her. "I will leave you to your treatment Lara. But let me first say that I am very proud of you. Very proud. You not only picked the correct remedy but your bedside manner was beyond reproach. You talked to your patient every step of the way, explaining to her what was going on... you would be surprised how many experienced Healers forget that to truly heal one must first empathise with the patient's fears. Well done."

Lara waited until her teacher had left and sat beside Elina. "Here," she said kindly, "drink all of this and then we will begin."

She watched as Elina drained the flask and smiled in surprise.

"Good huh?" Lara smiled. "I've never understood why medicines have to taste so bad when it's so easy to make them easier to swallow. Now lie back down and close your eyes. I am just going to pass my hands over you again, except this time I am going to send energy magic to you. Ready?"

Elina nodded and closed her eyes. Lara reached out her hands and let them hover a few centimetres away from Elina's body. She pulled on her own core, her essence, which Healer Thomas had taught them was the source of all their magicks, and let it flow through her like a conduit and into Elina. She controlled the flow of the magicks so as not to startle Elina. Soft silvery tendrils of magicks streamed out of her hands and wound themselves around Elina's body until she was covered in a cocoon of silver.

Lara watched in awe as the cocoon pulsated as though alive. She had never seen anything quite like it before. The magicks around Elina were so thick she couldn't even see her anymore. It wasn't quite what she had been expecting.

"Are you alright Elina?" she asked cautiously.

"I feel wonderful," Elina exclaimed. "I feel so warm and whole."

Lara waited, unsure of what to do next. Just when she was about to go and call Healer Thomas, the cocoon melted away as if it had never been there at all. Lara gasped.

"What is it?" Elina asked as she opened her eyes.

"Gods above!" Lara exclaimed.

"What?" Elina said. "I feel great."

Lara grabbed a mirror and held it in front of her. "Look!" she urged Elina.

Elina's mouth dropped open when she saw her reflection. The haggard sunken face of an old woman was gone—she looked young again. She patted her cheeks in disbelief, looking for the wrinkles that had been there previously—they were gone. Her silver eyes were no longer matte and lifeless, they shone as brightly as they had before she had been taken from her home.

She turned to Lara with tears in her eyes. "Thank you!" she exclaimed, clasping Lara's hands in her own. "Thank you!"

Lara shook her head. "I don't think I had much to do with it," she said confused. "I just made the potion as it said in the book... I only used a small amount of energy magicks... but you look so young... did I do something wrong? I don't think the spell was supposed to make you younger?"

Elina laughed for the first time in over a decade. "You have done nothing wrong Lara, you have not made me younger. I am twenty one. That is my true age. Your spell worked perfectly. What you saw before was from the effects of my captivity."

Lara frowned. "Elina who took you, who did those things to you?"

Elina's smile fell. "I cannot tell you that Lara. And you must speak of this to no one, do you understand?"

"But Elina, the person that kidnapped you must be caught and punished! You can't let them get away with it!"

"Don't worry Lara, they will get what they deserve in time... for now it is too dangerous for us to do anything about it."

Lara chewed her lip, lost in thought.

"Do not worry so," Elina smiled at her kindly. "What you have done for me today is cause for celebration... although I do not think it wise for others to see what you have achieved."

Lara looked at her questioningly.

"There are people out there who would like nothing better than to get their hands on one so powerful Lara... you must be wary of whom you trust, and not let others know how strong your magicks are... not yet at least."

"Dangerous? But my magicks are no more powerful than any other students," Lara said.

Elina shook her head. "You are wrong about that Lara."

They were interrupted by a knock at the door. It was Healer Thomas, come back to inspect Lara's treatment. He froze when he saw Elina—the shock clearly visible on his kind face. He looked at Elina and she nodded.

"Almighty Goddess," he sighed reverently. "I have never seen anything like it!" He turned to Lara. "Amazing!"

Lara flushed.

Healer Thomas examined Elina more closely, muttering to himself as he did. "Lara, this is truly beyond what I believed possible... it is almost miraculous."

"But I just did an energy spell..." Lara said confused.

Healer Thomas looked at her. "Lara, this is amazing... and I am sorry to ask you this, but I want you to tell no one about this... not a word."

"But won't they see it for themselves when Elina comes back for her next treatment?" she asked.

Healer Thomas smiled, "Lara, I don't think you understand... you have cured her—there is no need for other treatments!"

"But you said there was no cure for what had happened to Elina?"

"There isn't... which is why you need to keep this to yourself... I don't want you attracting unwanted attention to either yourself or to Elina for that matter."

Lara nodded. "Of course Sir, I know the patient confidentiality agreement anyway."

"Good girl. You must be tired by now. Why don't you go and join your friends for lunch? I will see Elina away safely and tidy up later."

Lara nodded and with a quick wave to Elina she left the healing chamber.

"Now do you see what I am saying?" Elina said to Healer Thomas.

"Yes," he scratched his long silvery beard. "I am beginning to understand—it is more important than ever that she be taught how to control her magicks... we must keep her hidden until the time is right."

***

Lara waved at her friends from the lunch queue. They were already sitting waiting for her.

"So?" Leyla asked her excitedly when she sat down with her tray. "How did it go? I heard that you got chosen to see the first patient!"

Lara nodded. "It was great! It felt so right, like I was doing what I was meant to..." She looked around. "I'll tell you more about it later though..."

Anna laughed, "Spoken like a true healer! My granddad is a healer too, that's how he talks. 'Anna,'" she mimicked her grandfather's deep voice, "healing is not a career, it is a vocation—a calling."

Lara smiled. "Laugh all you like, he's right... it's as if my magicks know what they need to do without me even being aware of it. I just knew what to do, I don't know how I knew but I just did."

"Instinct," Sofia said. "All of our magicks are tied into our instincts and emotions—think of it like a subconscious awareness."

"Ooh, someone's been reading up on their magical histories again!" Anna teased her. "Who knew it was such a fascinating subject?" She winked. "Or is it the teacher you find so fascinating?"

Sofia blushed slightly. "Mr Aldric is a great teacher! I'm really enjoying History of Magic this year." She winked at Lara and Leyla, "Although it doesn't hurt that he's cute too!"

The four friends were still chatting as they finished their lunch and walked to their next class which happened to be Magical Histories. Sofia was so busy staring at Mr Aldric that she never saw Jayla stick her foot out as she passed. She tripped and fell to the floor, knocking her head on one of the desks.

Lara glared at Jayla as she smirked at Sofia's misfortune.

"Oh dear!" Jayla exclaimed with false concern. "Poor Sofia, so clumsy, are you alright?"

Lara knelt down to pick Sofia up. Her head was bleeding a fair bit. She turned to Jayla and whispered so no one else could hear, "Mess with any of my friends again and you will be sorry."

Jayla was about to respond when she saw the look on Lara's face. She recoiled slightly at the ice in Lara's eyes. As she looked at Lara, mesmerised by her eyes, she noticed something strange—Lara's pupils flickered and turned into slits, the pale blue of her eyes suddenly turning an almost black blue colour. She blinked and looked again, but Lara's eyes were the same as they had always been.

"Whatever!" she said, turning away from Lara with an attempt to disguise her disconcertment.

Lara helped Sofia to her seat, she glanced around the room quickly to make sure no one was watching and then covered the gash on Sofia's forehead with her palm.

"What are you...?" Sofia stilled as a slight warm feeling seeped into the cut on her head numbing the pain. A deep feeling of contentment passed through her.

"Lara!" Anna exclaimed, as the deep gash on Sofia's forehead knit itself back together. "That's amazing!"

"Shh!" Lara warned her, "Don't say a word about it... I'll explain it all to you later."

"Thanks!" Sofia said as she felt her smooth forehead.

"Good afternoon class!" Mr Aldric said enthusiastically. "I hope you are all well and ready for today's class! Today we are going to learn about the creation of Azmantium—it is one of the most interesting topics on our syllabus."

He raised his hands in the air and the lights dimmed. He executed a series of swirls in the air and a large holographic image of a planet appeared.

"This is Azmantium. Now you might notice that it looks very different in this image. That is because this is how our planet looked millennia ago. We don't have a way of knowing what it looked like at the start of its creation but this is the first recorded picture of the planet." He spun his fingers around the image and the globe began to turn slowly. "Notice how much darker the skies were back then," he said, pointing out the almost black purple of the skies. "Can anyone tell me why it was so dark?"

Sofia's hand shot up from the back row.

"Yes?" he asked, looking at her.

"It was because the second sun had not been born yet," she said shyly.

"Yes! That's right!" he exclaimed. "In the beginning Azmantium only had one sun. That is also why our planet used to be green. All of the plants and grass were green instead of the blue they are today due to the low levels of sunlight emanating from the sun."

He flicked his fingers and the image morphed into a different view.

"This is an image of our planet today. Note the different colours of the landscape."

The class all listened, rapt.

"The continents seem different too, why is that?" Sofia asked.

Mr Aldric smiled at her, his dark hair falling slightly into his green eyes. "That is an excellent question Sofia!"

He manipulated the globe again and it split into two.

"This one," he said pointing at the first image, "is how Azmantium looked before. The other is how it is today. The difference between the contours of the land masses is quite noticeable." He shook his head slightly. "This wasn't caused by the sun though, or any other natural evolution... this is the result of the Great War."

"The Great War?" Lara's friend Max asked.

Mr Aldric nodded. "I am sure that you have all heard about the Great War from your parents. Over a thousand years ago there was a terrible war... it lasted for many years..."

"What caused the war?" Xan asked with interest.

"No one is entirely sure of the answer to that one," Mr Aldric replied. "There are many different theories out there. Some say the witches started the war to get more power, others say the fey wanted to rule supreme over the world... suffice it to say that whoever started it, and whatever they were after, in the end all of the races became dragged into it. Different factions formed, and in their quest for power they almost destroyed Azmantium in its entirety." His eyes glazed over, "Magicks filled the air ripping apart the very molecules of the planet... Friends turned on friends, racism thrived."

"How did the war end?" Anna asked.

"It was a fey called Meriel who finally managed to end the war. He called for peace and solidarity in a time when people were beginning to get desperate. Everyone lived in fear. He was an exceptionally strong fey who used his magicks and cunning to heal the rifts between the races."

"Wasn't he the first King?" Xan asked.

Mr Aldric nodded. "That is right. In fact Xan, I guess that makes him your great, great, great... grandfather. We owe him much to be honest... if he had not intervened we might not have Azmantium today."

"Exterminating some of the vermin like the shifters doesn't sound so terrible to me," Jayla whispered to her friends.

Mr Aldric's smile disappeared, replaced by a harsh look no one had ever seen on his usually sunny face before.

"Would you like to repeat what you just said Jayla?" he said calmly.

Jayla flushed bright red as she realised that he had heard her comment.

"I... I was just joking..." she stuttered.

"You should never joke about such matters. Intolerance of others and of those different from us is what caused the war in the first place." He glared at her until she looked down. "Anyway," he continued, "we have gotten off topic." He flicked the hologram again and it reverted to the first image of Ancient Azmantium. "So, how did the races first come to be?"

He looked around the class. "We have a variety of different races living on this planet today—how did they come to exist? Who was here first? These are questions we do not have the answers to yet. For next week's assignment

I want you all to research the topic and to write me an essay about how and why the races came into existence."

"But you just said there were no answers?" Lara said questioningly.

He nodded. "Exactly, so there can be no wrong answers... I want you to do your research and write about your own theories. But, although theories are not fact, they do need to be supported by some historical evidence." He snapped his fingers and a sheet appeared on each desk. "Here is a list of books you may find useful. And please, I know it is a fascinating subject and that your imaginations will likely run wild, but please try to keep it as scientific and realistic as possible—this is a history class not creative writing," he reminded them as they started to file out of the classroom.

CHAPTER 8

Later that night Lara sat at her desk reading about the history of Azmantium. Leyla was already fast asleep in her room as was everyone else judging by the lack of chatter in the dorm wing. Lara stared at the book in front of her, deep in thought. Earlier that evening she had told the girls what had really happened in the healing chamber, well, everything except the part about Elina's past and traumatic memories—that was personal and not hers to tell. She had sworn them to secrecy about her excessive ability to heal. She knew she could trust them.

What she hadn't told them though was of her worries. Something was off, she could sense it with every fibre of her being, but she didn't know what it was. She tried to focus on the chapter she was reading about the first races on the planet but the words began to swim around on the page. She yawned, closed the book and headed to her room. She sank gratefully down on her soft bed, barely managing to get under the covers before sleep took her.

"Larissa... Lara..." a voice called to her.

Lara opened her eyes and looked around. She was not in her bedroom at magic school, she was in a blue field filled with fragrant red flowers. She blinked a few times. The colours around her seemed off, as if she were seeing through someone else's eyes.

"Lara, come find me," the gently voice called out again. "I am waiting for you."

Lara walked in the direction the voice was coming from as though on autopilot. She walked for a long while until she came to a pale green stream, its waters dancing in the silver moonlight.

"You know how to find me... feel the earth around you..." the voice urged.

Lara crossed the stream, the cool waters lapping at her ankles as she waded through, and walked through a clearing in the lush blue forest until she came upon a well hidden cave behind a clump of trees. She walked inside fearlessly, sensing no danger. The cave was larger than it had seemed from the outside. Huge cavernous walls of silver stone glistened with evening dew and white crystals clung to the cave roof. A variety of tunnels led off from the main entrance. Lara followed a soft glow of light coming from one of the tunnels in front of her.

After making her way through a series of interconnected tunnels she finally came to a large blue wood door. She instinctively pushed it open and went in. A beautiful woman was sitting in front of a large log fire shooting off blue sparks. Her long golden hair fell down her back in waves complementing the golden hue of her skin. She looked up at Lara with big blue eyes.

"Welcome Lara, I have been waiting for you for a very long time."

Lara looked at the beautiful vision in front of her in awe. "Who are you?" she asked.

"Come, sit down by the fire with me," the lady said, patting a large silk cushion next to her.

Lara did as she was told. Her vision was still playing tricks on her, everything seemed brighter than possible, first the flowers in the field and now this lady before her. She looked up to find the lady watching her with a tender expression on her face.

"It is good to see you, Lara," she smiled. "I have waited a long time to meet you."

"Who are you?" Lara asked again. "You look familiar."

The lady nodded. "Your senses are telling you that you know me, and they are not wrong... I am Asena."

"How do I know you?" Lara asked, accepting the cup of tea Asena handed her.

"You were not yet born when I saw you last," Asena said. "Yet we are two of a kind, like recognises like..."

Lara shook her head confused. "I don't understand... how did you see me if I wasn't born yet?"

Asena smiled at her gently. "Child, there is much I cannot tell you yet... I called you here to me so that we could finally meet. I need you to know that I am always with you even when you cannot see me... I have always been with you ever since you were born." She put a hand on Lara's shoulder. A great sense of peace and warmth flowed into Lara with Asena's touch—something fluttered inside of her, urging her to lean into Asena.

Asena stroked her hair while Lara rested her head on her shoulder. She hummed a song while Lara closed her eyes—some part of her recognising the song she was hearing, feeling a great sense of having come home. They sat like that for a while, both enjoying each other's proximity until Asena broke the peaceful silence.

"You must go now child, and return to your own world."

"I wish I could stay here longer, stay with you," Lara said, sitting up reluctantly.

"As do I," Asena said wistfully, "but you know the way here now, you can come to see me whenever you wish to. But I need you to make me a promise Lara."

Lara looked at her expectantly.

"You must be careful," Asena urged her. "I know you do not yet understand, but you are special… more special than you can imagine. There are those that would seek to use you for your powers."

"I'm just a healer," Lara said. "I don't understand why anyone would want to bother with me."

"Oh child," Asena sighed. "You are much more than 'just' a healer… I must not say too much, it is too soon… I will be watching you from afar… but if you need anything, anything at all you must call to me… and I will come."

She pulled Lara into a warm embrace and gently kissed the top of her head. "Walk in the light my child."

Lara woke up disorientated. She was back in her own bed at magic school. She could hear Leyla singing in the shower and the red sunlight was already streaming through her windows. She looked at the time and almost fell out of bed in her rush to get up. She snatched some clothes off the chair by the wall and quickly pulled a brush through her hair and splashed some water on her face.

"Oh, you're finally up!" Leyla said as she came into her room towelling her hair.

"It's late! Why didn't you wake me up?" Lara asked her as she hurriedly packed her books in the bag.

Leyla laughed. "Are you kidding? I tried everything to wake you up... it was like you were in a coma. That's what you get when you go to bed so late studying all night!"

"I didn't stay up that late..." Lara trailed off.

"Well, at least you look rested," Leyla said looking at her.

"I feel great," Lara mused.

"You probably needed the sleep... although, please don't do that again! You were so still I actually checked you were still breathing you know! C'mon let's go get some breakfast before class."

Lara followed her downstairs lost in thought. It had to have been a dream...

***

Meanwhile, in a hidden wing of the castle-like magic school Elder Aelwen was in a meeting. She paced the length of the dark subterranean chamber. A cloaked figure sat on the dark purple sofa opposite her.

"Things are moving forward faster than we had predicted," Aelwen worried. "I thought we had more time."

The figure nodded. "As did I Aelwen. But Healer Thomas's reports speak for themselves... she is coming into her powers faster than we had anticipated. You heard how she healed Elina—it just should not be possible at this point, but she did it... I have never seen such a transformation in one so ill... and an Oracle to boot. Young Lara has no idea of the power she wields."

Aelwen leaned against the silver stone wall and sighed. "There must be something we can do? Maybe if we bound her powers again? We might be able to slow down the transformation."

"I am afraid that we are not powerful enough to bind her powers."

"But we did it once!" Aelwen protested.

"Yes, but she was only a baby, a new born at the time… and if you remember as I do, even then it took all of us at maximum strength to even partially bind them." The cloaked figure shook his head. "I am afraid that is no longer an option."

"Then what do we do?" Aelwen asked. "At this rate she will be discovered in a matter of weeks, months if we're lucky. Do we hide her away somewhere away from school?"

He shook his hooded head, "I am afraid that is no longer possible Aelwen. News of Lara has already reached Merrick."

Aelwen froze. "How? We hid the extent of her healing powers!"

"I know. But you know the King has spies everywhere… and it was not her healing powers that were mentioned to him."

"Then why has he heard of her?" Aelwen said confused.

"I believe a certain young prince's attention is the reason for the King's interest," he said. "Young Xan is by all accounts, smitten with our young charge."

"They are only children, why should the King care about that?!" she exclaimed.

"The King is a strategist my dear, and according to the rumours Xan is his favourite son. It would be naïve to think that he would not have Lara investigated."

Aelwen slumped on a chair, tired of pacing. "What do we do now then?"

"We prepare for the inevitable—we always knew it would eventually come to this... and we pray that Lara's secret stays safe a while longer." He stood up and walked over to where she was sitting. "Don't worry so," he said gently, putting a hand on her shoulder. "We are not alone in this. Every day our numbers grow and Elina has taken a real liking to Lara, she has promised to talk to the other Oracles about joining our cause."

"How will she even find them? They are in hiding and have been for decades... and she has only recently escaped herself. How will she know where to look?"

He shrugged. "I did not ask... you know how secretive Oracles can be, but she assured me that she knows where they are. She thinks once they hear about Lara they will want to help."

Aelwen nodded with renewed vigour. "I will talk with the others, they can spread the word. We must be prepared..."

The cloaked figure nodded and walked to the hidden door behind the bookcase. He turned before he left and looked at Aelwen wistfully. "I wish I could stay a while longer dear heart, but the King demands my presence tonight."

She nodded with a small smile.

"Aelwen, the most important thing you can do right now is to teach Lara extreme control over her powers… If she is as smart and powerful as you all say we might be able to hide her a while longer."

*****

"So, you're what all the fuss is about," a tall boy said, coming to stand in front of Lara.

Lara looked up. There were two almost identical looking dark haired boys blocking her way. They looked so much like Xan that they had to be the brothers she had heard about from Anna and Sofia.

"Little brother has good taste," the slightly shorter one smirked.

"Allow us to introduce ourselves," the taller one said. "I am Seth and this is Darren."

Lara nodded. "You're Xan's brothers."

"That we are," Darren, the middle brother said, draping his arm around Lara's shoulders.

She tried to hide her instinctive reaction to his touch which was to recoil. He didn't seem to notice though as he kept his arm there as they walked along.

"I hear you already met Jayla," Darren snickered. "I'm sorry I wasn't there to see what happened."

Seth grinned at Lara. "So am I. Oh, to have been a fly on the wall and to have seen her face when you doused her with water and threw her in the air."

"That's not quite what happened…" Lara tried to interject.

94

"Don't worry about it," Seth said, sidling next to her. "The way I see it, she deserved what she got."

"But isn't she your girlfriend?" Lara asked surprised at his reaction.

"One of them at least!" Darren high-fived his brother. "Although between you and me he needs to be a little more careful with that one, her father is an Elder and happens to be our father's closest friend." He looked at Seth speculatively. "Dear father would be ever so upset if Seth were to ruin the future father has all mapped out for him."

Seth glared at his brother and then turned to Lara. "So Lara, tell me about yourself."

Lara shrugged, uncomfortable with Xan's brothers. They all looked so alike and yet while they were all undeniably handsome, these two had a hardness around their dark brown eyes while Xan's hazel ones were sincere.

"There's not much to tell actually," she said.

"Oh, come now," Darren cajoled. "There's no need to be so humble... I hear you are quite the Healer."

"Yes, you even managed to impress Elder Akkarin... the Gods only know how hard it is to achieve that," Seth looked at her with interest.

"It wasn't a big deal really," Lara tried to step away from Darren's grip on her shoulder. She could feel a flutter in her stomach, the same feeling she had when her magicks were about to manifest. She had to control it though, she had promised Aelwen.

"There you are Lara, I have been looking all over for you!" Xan exclaimed as he came up behind them. The look in his eyes belied the cheeriness of his voice but his brothers didn't seem to notice.

"Well, look at that, lover boy is here!" Seth said loudly.

Xan rolled his eyes at him. "Hardly, we're just friends Seth."

Lara looked at him gratefully as he jostled Darren away from her.

"Sorry guys, we have a study group to get to at the library," Xan said as he took Lara's book bag.

"Aw, we were just getting to know Lara too..." Seth pouted.

"Another time maybe," Xan called over his shoulder as he dragged Lara away from them. "Oh, and by the way Seth, Jayla was looking for you... she didn't seem very happy when I saw her."

Xan slowed his pace once Seth and Darren were out of sight. "Are you Ok? Did they upset you?" he asked.

Lara shook her head. "No, it's fine. They are a bit full on though."

"That's one way of putting it," he sighed. "Sometimes I feel like the older brother even though they're sixteen and fifteen."

"Well, you're only a year younger than Darren... although I see what you mean about the mental age."

He smiled. "They don't mean anything by it, they just like to mess around... I'm sorry if you were uncomfortable though."

"That's ok."

"So are you coming to the study group?" he asked her.

She looked surprised. "You were serious about that?"

He nodded. "A few of us get together twice a week to study. Exams are in a few weeks you know."

"Okay, let's go... as long as Jayla isn't one of your study buddies!" she laughed as they walked to the library.

CHAPTER 9

"Are you sure this is a good idea?" Lara asked as Anna and Sofia joined her and Leyla in their room.

"Yes, this is the best time to look!" Anna said. "It's easier to see the glimmer of magicks when it's dark."

Lara looked unsure. "How much trouble will we get in if we get caught wandering through the school at night?"

"Don't worry!" Sofia whispered. "I have an invisibility charm... we will be fine!" Sofia held up an ornately engraved silver locket. "I got this from Deedee's shop of the Wonderfully Weird. Deedee said that it is a level four strength cloaking charm. No one is going to be expecting it."

"How on earth did you get such a powerful charm?" Leyla asked with awe. "It must have cost a fortune!"

Sofia shrugged. "I help Deedee out at the shop during the holidays. It makes me some extra pocket money and it helps her out as it's the busiest time of year for her... she gave me this as a thank you."

Lara looked at the locket dubiously. "How is it going to work? Will it make all four of us invisible or just the wearer?"

"Once I activate it, it will basically link us all to the locket… whoever is wearing it gets to decide who is included in the charm." Sofia slipped it around her neck. "C'mon guys, let's go!"

They crept to the door and watched as Sofia pressed the centre stone on the locket. A soft purple light undulated out of the gem and twined itself around each of the girls. Leyla looked at Lara.

"I can still see you. I don't think the charm worked!"

Sofia pulled Leyla in front of the mirror on the wall. "Look!" she said.

Leyla gasped as she looked in the mirror—she didn't have a reflection!

"We can still see each other because we are linked through the spell," Sofia whispered. "But no one else can see us."

Anna opened the door to the dorm and peered out. "Right everyone, the coast is clear. Remember though, no one can see us but they can still hear us, so be as quiet as you can!"

They tiptoed out of the room in a line and made their way along the dark hallway and down the stairs to the main hall. Lara was so busy looking around that she stepped on Leyla's foot.

"Sorry!" she whispered.

Leyla nodded.

"Where do we start looking?" Anna asked Sofia.

"Let's start here in the main hall, it's the perfect place to hide a secret passage door or tunnel, look how many doors lead off from it," Sofia said. "Lara you search the north section, Leyla you the east, Anna can look at the west and I'll take the south. Remember if you find something don't call out!!"

The girls nodded and each walked across the massive hall chamber to their section. Lara felt a wave of cold course through her as she quietly made her way to the north of the room passing by the rows of imposing statues lining her way. She looked up. She could have sworn that they were watching her. She quickened her pace. The last statue was that of the first King, Meriel. She paused briefly in front of it, remembering Mr Aldric's words from class about how he had united the races. Just as she started to turn away to continue on her path she noticed a slight movement from the corner of her eye. When she turned back to King Meriel's statue it seemed to her that he was standing in a slightly different pose than before. She inched closer to inspect the statue—it was still. She shook her head at her flight of fancy—great, now she was imagining things; the girls were going to have a field day with this.

She turned to head to the north and stumbled. She instinctively held her hands out to grab the closest thing to stabilise herself and found herself gripping the base of King Meriel's statue. Adrenaline coursed through her at her near accident, her heart beating double time.

"I have been waiting for this day for a long time," a deep voice said, startling her.

Lara jumped in her skin and looked around, searching for the owner of the voice. The stone of the statue vibrated beneath her hand and she looked up to find two glowing eyes staring down at her.

"How…?" she whispered.

"I am sorry if I frightened you," the King said kindly. *"I have been hoping for a chance to talk with you awhile."*

"But you're… you're…"

He nodded. *"Yes child, I am dead… I died many centuries ago, at least my body did."*

Lara looked at him puzzled.

"Before I died I performed a ritual… the Karhan. You will not have heard of it as I made sure that any and all mentions of the Karhan were struck from the official records and books—it is as though it never existed."

"What is the Karhan?" Lara asked intrigued. "And why did you erase it from history?"

He sighed. *"The Karhan is a ritual that can only be performed by the most powerful of beings… it is a process which enables the subject's essence to remain alive—a sort of immortality if you will."*

"You've been conscious all this time? You've lived through centuries of other people's lives as a statue?" Lara was appalled. "Why would anyone want to do that?"

"It is not a question of 'want' but rather of 'need.' I had to undergo the ritual…" he paused and sighed. *"I will not lie to you. It has been hard being aware of all that goes on around me all these years. I have seen many distressing things happen since my death. It should not shock me really… for this was all foretold."*

"What was foretold?" Lara asked.

"The darkness infecting our world… it has been a long time coming, and I am very much afraid that despite my best efforts to unite the races and bring about peace the darkness is spreading."

"But you succeeded," Larissa exclaimed. "Witches, vampires, fey... they're all living together in harmony."

He shook his head. *"On the surface perhaps... but there is trouble brewing. When I was still alive my closest friend was an Oracle called Sage. He predicted that the darkness would rise once again..."* he paused as though remembering. *"He predicted many things which I will not go into at the moment—but what he saw is the reason I chose to undergo the Karhan. I knew this day would come, I have remained on Azmantium in order to help battle the dark."*

"Does anyone else know you are here?" Lara asked.

He shook his head.

"Why tell me?" she asked. "I don't understand why you chose to speak to me."

The old King smiled down at her. *"You are the one Lara, you will lead us to a new era of light and hope."*

Lara backed away slightly from the statue. "I'm just an almost thirteen year old in her first year at magic school, how can I do anything about the darkness? I think you have me confused with someone else!"

"I am sorry to burden you with such knowledge Lara," the King sighed sadly, *"but I think it is always better to know the truth than to hide behind a lie. You know there is something different about you—you can sense it... the time is coming when you will need to come to terms with what you really are."*

"Lara!" Leyla whispered loudly in her ear and poked her in the ribs.

Lara stared at Leyla.

"Geez, I have been trying to get your attention for ages!! Come on, Anna found something!"

Lara turned to the statue, it was inert again—with no signs that it had ever been otherwise. She followed Leyla to where Sofia and Anna were waiting.

"Look!" Anna exclaimed, pointing at a tapestry hanging on the wall. Lara looked carefully at it. The edges of the fabric had a barely visible soft yellow glow around them. "It's one of the secret doors, I just know it!" Anna said excitedly.

Sofia grabbed one corner of the tapestry and lifted it—there was nothing there except a stone wall. She sighed with disappointment. "I was sure we had found it!" she huffed.

Leyla touched the wall. "I think we have found it, look!" she said grabbing Sofia's hand and passing it over the smooth surface of the stone. "Can you feel that?"

Sofia's face brightened instantly. "Yes!! The stone is smooth and cold but here in the middle," she patted the wall, "it's rough and warm… there's something here!"

"Of course!" Anna exclaimed. "They've hidden it with a concealment spell… Well, it wouldn't really be a secret passageway if it was obvious!"

"How do we open it though?" Leyla asked, patting the wall all over, trying to see if tapping a certain part would open the invisible door.

"It's bound to have some sort of lockspell on it," Sofia mused. "I don't have anything that would undo one of those."

"I was really looking forward to getting in too!" Anna exclaimed.

Sofia grinned. "And we will! I'm working at the shop this weekend, I'll see if I can't get an opener charm! And now that we know where it is we can find it easily!"

Footsteps echoed down the long hall.

"Shh!" Leyla said, "Someone's coming!"

The girls backed up against the wall and stood as still as the hall statues as they held their breath. The steps drew closer. Sofia and Anna had closed their eyes, as if that would somehow make them less visible.

"The King is coming?" a voice asked. It was Healer Thomas's voice.

"Yes," Aelwen replied as they walked slowly through the huge hall chamber. "He is due to arrive next week."

"Do you know why he's coming?" Thomas asked.

Aelwen shook her head. "No old friend... Elder Akkarin only told me that he is coming next week... and something about him paying an unofficial visit to the school, just to 'get a sense of things' as he put it."

"Do you think he knows something is going on?"

"He can't possibly... we have been more than careful."

"Do you think he is coming for her?" Thomas stopped walking and searched Aelwen's eyes.

"I doubt it... no one knows about her, not yet. I wonder if this all has something to do with him choosing his official heir... I have heard rumours that he has decided it is time to make it official—in case anything were to happen to him."

Healer Thomas snorted, "Like anything could kill that man. Besides, everyone already knows that Seth is going to be his chosen heir—he has been grooming him for the job for long enough!"

"Not necessarily," Aelwen mused. "King Merrick is a complex man, and very unpredictable… also I have heard that he is not happy with Seth right now, although I don't know why."

"Possibly because he's finally realised his eldest born is somewhat lacking in tact and intellect?" Healer Thomas quipped.

Aelwen smiled. "You really don't have a high opinion of him do you?"

Thomas shook his head. "Nor of his brother Darren, don't forget I taught them both in their first years." He shuddered, "And I thank the Gods every day that passes that neither of them continued with healing classes… two people more unsuited to the fine art of healing I have never met!"

"What about Xan?" she asked him. "You've been teaching him for two years now, what do you make of him?"

"He seems different than his brothers," Thomas scratched his beard. "He is polite and studious, friendly with most of his classmates… but I don't know Aelwen… he is still one of them. I have not yet decided what to make of him."

Aelwen nodded. "Fair enough. But remember not to judge him by his family Thomas, everyone deserves a fair chance."

He nodded and they walked on, passing by right next to where the girls were huddled against the wall.

"Phew!" Sofia exclaimed once they had left the hall. "I thought they would never leave!"

"I know!" Leyla agreed. "I was about to run out of oxygen!"

"Come on, let's get back to our rooms before we get found out," Lara said tiptoeing towards the staircase.

"So the King is coming here!" Anna exclaimed. "It's so exciting! I wonder if we'll get to meet him?"

"Probably not," Sofia said. "He's probably just coming to see his sons."

"Still... it's exciting all the same!" Anna enthused as they made their way back upstairs.

Ela Lourenco

CHAPTER 10

"Good morning Sofia!" Deedee, owner of the shop of the Wonderfully Weird, exclaimed.

Lara tried not to stare at the hulk of a woman standing in front of her. She was huge, layers of multi-coloured chiffon fluttering with each move she made, arms laden with a variety of mismatched bangles and charms. Thick set glasses making her eyes seem disproportionately large in her moon-shaped face.

"Hi Deedee!" Sofia said, returning her hug.

Lara looked at Leyla—who was not managing to hide her shock and was watching Deedee with her mouth open. She nudged her discreetly and gestured with her eyes. Leyla nodded in thanks and stopped staring.

"You've met Anna before," Sofia said, "but these are my new friends Lara and Leyla."

Deedee turned to them and clasped their hands, "Welcome girls, any friends of Sofia's are always welcome here!"

Leyla and Lara smiled at Deedee in return.

"Do you mind if my friends stay while I work my shift?" Sofia asked her.

Deedee shook her head effusively, the beads on the ends of her many tiny plaits bouncing with the movement. "Of course not! The more the merrier I always say. Beside it will give me a chance to get to know them, and give them a chance to have a look around." She grinned, her face suddenly seeming much younger, "I am sure they will find things they never even knew they needed!"

Sofia followed Deedee to the storeroom at the back of the shop leaving the three friends alone.

"Wow!! She is something else!" Leyla said once they were out of earshot.

Anna smiled, "She certainly is... she likes to make an impression!"

Lara walked around the shop. From the outside the shop seemed small and narrow but it was anything but... it was huge and just as quirky as its owner. A large room filled with stacks and shelves of things in every nook and cranny, with a multitude of arches leading off of it into separate alcoves of varying shapes and sizes. Amulets were draped on small pegs around the walls and cloaks in every colour and hue hung boldly on magically suspended racks in the air, drifting slowly across the shop as if preening their finery.

Leyla followed her into one of the larger alcoves off the main room. "Wow!" she murmured, "Deedee must have every herb and plant known to man!"

Lara nodded as she took in the rows of surprisingly neatly labelled wooden drawers on the walls. It was like a treasure trove for potion-makers and spell casters. She inhaled deeply as one of the incense burners lit itself and the sweet scent of apple blossom drifted into the room.

"Great advertising isn't it?" Deedee said coming up behind them. "I've spelled all the burners in the shop to light up with a different scent—they're motion-activated," she said proudly. "It's one of my finer achievements!"

"So they sense when someone's there and just light up by themselves?" Leyla asked in wonder.

Deedee nodded. "They're even spelled to burn whatever scent it thinks that specific person will like." She turned to Leyla, "You like apple blossom right?"

Leyla nodded mystified.

"You entered the room first, that's why it lit your scent."

"That's amazing!" Leyla exclaimed, "I thought it was random!"

Deedee turned to Lara, "Now, Lara, come and stand over here and it will pick your scent."

Lara stood where Deedee showed her, and a spicy scent mingled with a dash of something sweet and fragrant filled the air. Lara sniffed repeatedly. It smelt so familiar... and yet she couldn't put her finger on what the smell was. She turned to ask Deedee the name of the herb.

"What is that...?" she stopped mid-sentence as she caught sight of Deedee's face. The cheery smile had vanished, replaced by a look Lara could not decipher.

Deedee stared at Lara, frozen in place by the scent the burner had chosen for her. She looked Lara over—a tall, slim girl with deep blue eyes... eyes which seemed to hold a depth of wisdom and knowledge. She blinked as she saw Lara's pupils expand into slits momentarily... and then they were gone, back to normal. How could this be possible? How had she not known about this before? Deedee prided herself on two things in life—one was her shop, known to be the best stocked in all of Lantis, and the second was her extensive knowledge of all the goings-on everywhere on Azmantium. Sofia's mother Sarra, who worked as an intelligence officer for the King's guard, often joked that Deedee knew what was happening in the world before the King's elite officers did. It was a long standing joke that Deedee was the one to come to if anyone needed information—in fact as many people came for the info as they did for potions and spells.

"Deedee, what is it?" Lara asked.

Deedee forced a smile. "Nothing honey, I just remembered something I forgot to do yesterday... Mrs Crow had asked me to order some more marsh weed extract for her... I had better go and do it before I forget again!" She turned to leave.

"Deedee?" Lara said, "What was that scent it picked for me? I know that smell... I just can't remember what it is."

"And that's a shocker right there!" Leyla teased. "Seriously, you will never meet anyone who can remember scents and smells like Lara can!! She even beat the shifters in the class at the sniff test and they're supposed to be the best at it!"

Deedee paused for a moment and then smiled. "Do you know, I can't put my finger on it either... it is not a scent I have smelled for a while... I'll tell you what, I will look it up and let you know what it was next time I see you."

Lara nodded. She watched Deedee bustle away with the strangest sensation that Deedee had just lied to her about the scent—the question was, why?

***

"Here you go girls! Time for a break!" Deedee smiled as she set a giant plate of still warm cookies and a big pot of jasmine root tea on the small table behind the counter where she had a seating area with large comfy armchairs.

"Yum!" Sofia exclaimed, dusting off her hands before she reached for a cookie. "Elfberry choc chip, my favourite!"

"Really?" Deedee teased, "I hadn't noticed that in all the years I've known you... hmm, I guess that time when you were five and ate an entire batch by yourself when no one was looking and then had a stomach-ache for three days should have been an indication!"

Everyone laughed as Sofia pulled a face. "What can I say?" she pouted. "No one makes them like you do! Besides, you're the one that let me suffer when you had a potion you could have given me for the pain!"

Deedee smiled, "I wanted to sugar, but your mother wanted you to learn not to be so greedy next time! And there was nothing seriously wrong with you anyway." Deedee looked at Sofia as she shovelled three more cookies into her mouth. "Not that it seemed to have worked!" she said wryly.

Lara sipped at her tea—it was deliciously fragrant and sweet.

"Deedee, I have a favour to ask," Sofia said once she had finished the last cookie in her hand.

"Oh dear!" Deedee laughed. "I bet it's something your mother's not going to like!"

Sofia grinned, "Only if she finds out!"

Deedee threw her head back and laughed heartily, the many amulets and charms around her neck clinking together musically as she did. "Okay, what do you need this time?" she said, wiping a tear of mirth from her eyes.

"Well, two things actually..." Sofia fluttered her eyelashes innocently. "Firstly, I loved your concealment charm, and it was awesome! But it's run out now... I was wondering if you could recharge it for me?"

"Okay, and the second?" Deedee arched a brow.

"Well... we kind of need an opener spell... a powerful one, probably level four or five..."

Deedee stared at her, mouth agape. "Girl, what do you need such a powerful charm for? What exactly are you up to?" She looked at Sofia with her hands on her hips.

"Total deniability ... if you don't know you can't tell... or get into trouble with my mother. Think; if you know and I get caught then when mom asks you if you knew you will have to admit you did or lie to her... this way you can honestly say you didn't know what we were up to. I promise it's not for anything remotely dangerous. It's just for a bit of fun."

Deedee looked at each of the four girls in turn. "You promise me it's not for anything that can hurt you or others?"

They all nodded.

"You will be careful as to how you use it?" she asked, and they nodded again.

"Well, if you get caught you will deny any and all involvement on my part." Deedee laughed as Sofia threw herself at her and gave her a huge hug.

"Thanks Deedee, you're the best!!" Sofia said.

"Right, break time over," Deedee said gruffly as she put away the plates and cups. She never could say no to Sofia. She had never married nor had children of her own... Sofia was the daughter of her closest friend Sarra, and Deedee loved her as if she were hers.

While Sofia and Deedee went back to work, the girls continued their exploration of the shop.

"Look at this!" Anna exclaimed, holding up a small wooden figurine.

"What is it?" Leyla asked, examining it from all sides.

"It's a talisman for luck!" Anna explained. "This is made from Hila wood—Hila trees only grow in the most desolate places on the world. It is known for its boosting powers."

"So it amplifies powers?" Lara asked.

Anna nodded, "Once you've carved your Hila wood, you cast whichever spell you're using, which in this case is a luck spell, and the wood retains the spell and maximises it. They're used a lot in the Council. My mom's told me about them. I'm going to buy this one, exams are up soon and I think I am going to need all the luck I can get!"

Lara wandered off on her own leaving the two of them chatting. She walked under a low rise arch and came to a small alcove with a range of gleaming orbs of various sizes on display. She walked over to one of the shelves and picked up one of the smaller silver orbs, it was deceptively heavy for its small size and cold to the touch. She turned it over, carefully looking at it from all angles. It was perfectly smooth and round, there were no openings that she could see. She wondered what it was for. She put it back in its place and wandered through another archway into a small chamber. It was filled with numerous different items, from magnifying glasses, to sand timers and back scratchers. She smiled at the haphazardly filled room. A thin layer of dust covered the shelves, contrarily to the rest of the shop which was pristine.

"Ah, you've found my room of Odds and Ends!" Deedee exclaimed. She sneezed loudly. "Oh dear, I really must see that this room gets a good clean!"

"What is all this?" Lara asked.

"This is where I put all the gadgets that I don't know what to do with," she explained. "I spelled this room so that anyone who enters it will find what they are looking for."

Lara looked at her appreciatively. "I must not need anything then, as it didn't give me anything."

"Everyone needs something," Deedee smiled holding up the silver orb Lara had looked at previously.

Lara looked at her in astonishment. "How did you know I was looking at that?"

"It appeared on the counter with your name on it, see?" she said, showing Lara where her full name Larissa had engraved itself on the bottom. "That means that it has chosen you, it is yours."

"But what is it for?" Lara asked.

"It's called a 'globe of reflection'," Deedee explained. "It is used for deep meditation and for dream quests. They are not used as widely as they once were—which is a shame really as they are actually very powerful tools." She shrugged, "But you know what people are like, it's all about fashion and trend... today's treasure is tomorrow's junk and all that. And modern living has seen a move away from introspection and a move towards hip gadgets." She sighed, "It's such a shame that people don't take the time to really reflect on things anymore..." she trailed off, a distant look in her eyes.

Lara held the orb in her hand. It seemed to fit into her palm perfectly, as if it had been made for her.

"How much is it?" she asked Deedee, taking out her purse.

"Oh no! You can't pay for it!" Deedee said emphatically. "It has chosen you, it is yours."

"But..."

"No buts... I am a strong believer in kismet, fate... if an object in my shop chooses to belong to someone who am I to stand in the way? Although it may not always be clear in the beginning everything has a reason, a purpose." She closed Lara's hand over the orb. "Consider it a gift and use it wisely."

"I don't know how it works," Lara said questioningly.

"I will leave you to figure it out for yourself... I hear you are very smart." Deedee smiled at her over her shoulder as she went back to the counter to attend to her customers.

Lara put the globe in her bag and went in search of her friends. She found Leyla and Anna trying on ceremonial robes in a chamber at the back of the shop.

"Don't I look important?!" Leyla exclaimed as she twirled around in a dark green velvety robe which complemented her olive skin perfectly.

"It really suits you," Lara smiled.

"How about me?" Anna said, pirouetting in her dark red robe.

"You both look great," Lara smiled.

"Here, try this one on!" Leyla said putting an amazing twilight blue into her hands. "I bet you look great in it!"

Lara chuckled and pulled it on over her head. It fit her perfectly.

"Wow!" Anna said, "It really brings out your eyes!! I think you should get it, I think we all should, we are going to need dress robes for ceremonies and end of year parties anyway... it's the one uniform the school insists on."

Lara felt the soft velvet longingly. "Well... I do really like it..."

Anna clapped her hands. "Let's find one for Sofia to try on too!!" She started rummaging through the piles of robes. "Oh, look!! This dark purple one will look great with her hair! And it's her favourite colour too!"

They took their robes to the counter. Deedee was deep in conversation with an elderly gentleman. They were whispering furiously in a corner of the main room. Deedee was gesticulating wildly with her hands, bangles clanging furiously.

"Who's that?" Lara asked Sofia, who was minding the counter.

"Oh, that's Healer Riven, well, he used to be the head Healer, but he's retired now," Sofia said.

"Wait! That's *the* Healer Riven?" Lara gasped, looking back at him.

"Yeah," Sofia said as she admired the robe they had chosen for her. "He's a nice guy. He comes in regularly."

"He's more than a nice guy... he's a legend!" Lara enthused. "Did you know he invented the particle spell?!"

The girls looked at her blankly.

"You know!" Lara continued, "The spell that allows Healers to regrow lost limbs?"

"Would you like his autograph?" Anna joked.

"Do you think he would mind?" Lara said earnestly.

Deedee walked over to them with Healer Riven in tow. "Sofia could you get Healer Riven's package from the back please?" she said.

Sofia nodded and headed to the storeroom.

Lara stared at Healer Riven. He smiled down at her with kind green eyes, his face crinkling merrily.

"Hello," he said to the girls. "You must be Sofia's friends."

The girls nodded. He turned to Lara. "And you must be the talented young Healer I have heard so much about."

"Me?" Lara practically stuttered, "You've heard about me?"

He nodded, eyes twinkling. "Indeed I have, Healer Thomas has been singing your praises to me since the very beginning of term... and it is not easy to impress him you know."

"You know Healer Thomas?"

"Of course," he chuckled. "After all I taught him all those years ago when he was just a boy himself! He was my best student, although don't tell him I said that, he might get a big head!"

Leyla nudged Lara and jerked her head in encouragement.

"Sir," Lara said, "do you think you could, well... that is if you don't mind... I ... could I have an autograph?"

Deedee chuckled as Healer Riven took out some paper and a pen and signed it for Lara.

Lara looked at the note. *'Keep up the good work and become the Healer you know you can be, yours faithfully, Healer Riven.'*

"Thank you Sir!" Lara beamed at him.

"My pleasure Lara, it's not every day I get to meet the future of Healing," he said. He paid for his package, turned and gave a small bow to the girls and Deedee and then left.

"You do realise she's going to frame that and hang it on her wall, don't you?" Leyla teased.

Lara blushed, it was exactly what she had thought to do.

Deedee laughed heartily. "I can think of worse role models to idolise... at least she picked one for his deeds... unlike someone I know..." she looked at Sofia. "Someone whose idol happens to be the lead singer of a certain band called Foxed?"

Sofia blushed. "Hey, they make good music, and he's well, he's quite handsome."

Deedee patted her hand. "I hope you grow out of that one dear, last I heard he was evicted from the Gold Cauldron Hotel for trashing his room—not model behaviour." She turned to the girls, "So, you've picked your dress robes already? Good." She looked at their choices. "You have good taste ladies. Now, Sofia, why don't you wrap these up and call it a day? Go do something fun with your friends."

"Thanks Deedee!" Sofia said, quickly packaging the robes. "You're the best!"

"Oh, I almost forgot!" Deedee exclaimed, pulling something out of her pocket. "Here's your recharged concealment charm, and here is the level four opener spell," she looked at them intently. "Don't make me sorry I gave you these you hear?"

The girls nodded and hurried out of the shop.

Deedee flicked the closed sign on with a wave of her hand and sighed. It was beginning... she only hoped they would make it through the other side.

CHAPTER 11

"Yelena!" Lara called out as she unwarded the front door drawing a series of lock runes in the air.

The heavy door swung open as it recognised Lara's code and she walked in. She followed the noisy chatter from the kitchen and found her family in the kitchen baking—one of Yelena's favourite activities. She claimed it was relaxing, although Lara thought it had more to do with her sweet tooth.

No one heard her come in yet and she took the opportunity to watch them for a moment from the kitchen door. The entire house smelt of warm sugar and little Talia was covered in icing, from her hair to her rosy cheeks, doe brown eyes shining with excitement. Emmy and Sadie, who were eight and nine years old, were scattering glitter sugar on the cakes. Lara stifled a laugh as she saw Yelena sneak a bit of icing into her own mouth when she thought no one was looking.

"Will they be ready before Lara gets here?" Talia asked excitedly, rubbing her nose with the back of her hand and successfully covering that in icing too.

"They're almost done honey," Yelena said as Emmy and Sadie finished the last of the cakes and floated them over to the cupcake stand.

Yelena flicked her fingers and the mess in the kitchen vanished. "There," she said, "all done!" She looked at Talia who was now completely covered in pink and purple glitter icing and laughed.

"Oh, something smells good!" Lara exclaimed as she walked in and picked Talia up, twirling her in the air. "I think it's you... and I am so hungry... maybe I should take a bite?"

"Lara!" Talia squealed as Lara pretended to nibble at her. "You're home!!"

She hugged Lara tight, effectively covering her in icing too.

"Lara!" Yelena enveloped her in a big hug. "It's good to have you home honey, even if it is just for the weekend."

"I missed you so much!" Talia agreed, happily perched on Lara's lap, head snuggled into Lara's shoulder.

"I was only home five days ago!" Lara laughed.

Talia nodded solemnly, "Yes, a very long time!"

Lara bit into a cupcake and sighed with contentment.

"Good?" Talia asked.

"Delicious!" Lara exclaimed. "I think these are the best cakes I have ever eaten!"

"I made them!" Talia chirped. "Oh, Emmy and Sadie helped too."

Once everyone had eaten their fill and cleaned up Lara went to the back garden to play float the bubble with her foster sisters. Emmy and Sadie like to act all grown up most of the time but she knew that they also enjoyed the game Talia loved so much.

"Higher, go higher!!" Talia squealed as Lara and Sadie went head to head with their bubbles.

The point of the game was to blow a bubble, then capture it and race your opponent. The fastest bubble, as long as it didn't pop first, won the race, but you got extra points if you could manage to get multiple bubbles inside of the initial one. Lara had made the game up when Talia first came to live with them. She had been only two when her parents died—the cutest little toddler with big doe-like brown eyes filled with sorrow. Nothing would put a smile on her face, not even Yelena's soft touch had worked. One day though, Lara had been blowing bubbles in the garden and noticed Talia watching her from a distance. Encouraged by the first signs of interaction from her new little sister Lara had started messing around with the bubbles, using her magic and combining them, making them whizz through the air... and thus the 'float the bubble' game had been born. Talia had slowly come closer and closer to watch her, and eventually joined in. Ever since that day Talia had been like Lara's little shadow. You could rarely find one without the other. And although Lara loved all three of her sisters equally, she had a particularly soft spot for Talia.

Yelena watched from the kitchen window as her four girls played. As always Lara was subtly making sure that everyone had a turn and won a round although Lara was Lantis House's resident 'bubble master' as Talia liked to call it. She sighed as a low trill rang in her ear.

"Yes, Yelena here," she spoke quietly into the silver pendant around her neck which was in fact a charmed communication device.

"Yelena, it's Aelwen."

"Hi Aelwen, are you still coming over later for dinner?"

"I am, but I needed to talk to you without little ears around... can you talk?"

"Yes," Yelena nodded. "What is it?"

"The King is coming to magic school on Monday..."

Yelena paused. "I see... do you know why he's coming?"

"No," Aelwen frowned, "there is talk of him coming to evaluate his sons and pick an heir..."

"But you think it's more than that," Yelena stated.

"Frankly, yes. Why does he need to come to magic school to see his sons? He sees them every weekend— something else is going on."

Yelena thought for a moment. "Should we meet?"

"Yes, I have already contacted the others. We have arranged to meet late tonight... do you think you can make it?"

"Yes, Lara is home... she can watch the girls tonight. We will tell her we are going to see a late movie."

"Healer Thomas thinks we should tell Lara... I just wanted to tell you so you are warned before the meeting... and Yelena, he's not the only one."

"She's just a child!" Yelena answered with frustration. "Why can't we just let her be until it becomes necessary?"

Aelwen sighed, "Yelena, you know I care for Lara as if she were my own... my heart agrees with you, but my head... we should prepare her... anyway, we will discuss it later with the others."

"Alright," Yelena saw the girls coming in towards the house. "I have to go now, we'll talk later."

***

"That was amazing!" Lara patted her stomach. "I'm so full I'm going to burst!"

"Yelena wanted to make your favourite!" Talia chirped. "I told her it was triple cheese pizza!"

Lara laughed, "At this pace I'll be so big I won't be able to get through the door!"

Aelwen smiled. "Thank you Yelena. That was delicious as always."

Lara helped the girls clear the table and zapped the dishes clean and back into the cupboards.

"Lara, are you sure you'll be alright with the girls?" Yelena worried.

"Yes, we will be fine!" Lara said. "You go enjoy your movie. You don't get out often enough. Me and the girls are going to make popcorn and watch a holofilm ourselves."

Yelena took the coat Lara was holding out to her. "Well, okay, but call me if you need anything."

"I promise!" Lara laughed as she waved goodbye to them and closed the door.

***

Aelwen and Yelena walked up the long driveway to the house hidden behind a large cluster of trees. It was dark and no lights filled the torches standing sentry alongside the path. To the casual observer the house would seem abandoned. The façade of the house was derelict, with missing windows and tiles. The walls long since greyed with age and lack of care... that was all an illusion though. An illusion carefully maintained by the joint magicks of the group to mislead any seeking to spy on them. It was in fact a large castle-like house made of dark grey stone with imposing turrets standing proud at its four corners. It belonged to one of their own, although he didn't live there himself he made sure the house was well cared for—a sort of safe haven for their meetings.

Yelena shivered slightly as a damp mist descended. Aelwen walked up to the door and performed the sequence of runes that would allow them entry. A soft glow lit the porch briefly and the door shimmered and vanished until they were on the other side before rematerializing in place.

The house was deceptively well furnished on the inside. Long halls of gleaming Roxan wood led off to a myriad of rooms, each with a roaring fire in the fireplace and plush sofas. The two women walked past these chambers until they reached the wall at the end of the corridor. This time Yelena deactivated the wards spelling the wall and a large opening became visible, once again disappearing as they passed. They walked down four flights of steep stairs, the air growing heavy as they made their descent. Floating candles lit the way into the dark bowels of the house, gently leading them on their path.

Aelwen pushed open the heavy iron door when they finally got there. She glanced around the room. Everyone was there except for him- but they already knew that he wasn't coming. He had been summoned once again. She sat on a chair by the fireplace, the soft flicker of flames staving off the chill from the damp. Yelena sat on the other side and waited expectantly.

"Thank you all for coming," Aelwen said as she nodded in turn to each of the others. "I know that we were not to meet for a while, but there have been some new developments which have made this meeting necessary."

"I have already caught the others up on current events," Healer Thomas said.

"Thank you Thomas. That will save some time," Aelwen smiled. She turned to the others. "We, the Priests of the First, have been waiting a long time for this day to arrive." She looked at Yelena, "Our predecessors, who in their wisdom formed this group, would be proud to see how far we have come and how extensive our network is today." She paused briefly. "We have watched and waited for centuries, helping those we could, increasing our support with others like us who question the rightness of the path Azmantium is on. But the time has come now to come out of the shadows and to act."

She lifted a chalice filled with a golden liquid and took a sip, passing the cup over to Yelena. Once each member had drunk from the Chalice of Fire it was returned to Aelwen who put it back on the mantelpiece. It was still full to the brim although they had all had some as it was no ordinary chalice—it was the chalice given to the very first priest by the Goddess herself. It was imbued with the Goddess's own essence and refilled itself by magic each time it was emptied. The members of the priesthood were each given a boost in power and clarity from the golden liquid magicks, although they were careful not to take too much.

"The first matter we need to address is that of Leyla," Aelwen turned to Lily and Kieran, Leyla's parents. "We have successfully amended her registration records, so there is no need to fear on that account. However, it will be difficult to hide her powers for very long as they are growing at an alarming rate."

Lily nodded. "I realise that... we have been slowing her powers' progress somewhat with some ancient spells..." she looked at Aelwen and sighed. "If only I had been watching her more carefully..."

Kieran patted her knee, "It's no one's fault Lily."

When Leyla was still just a baby Lily had brought her to one of the group's meetings. She had only taken her eyes off of her for one minute and somehow Leyla had managed, at the tender age of eight months to transport the chalice to herself, and had then proceeded to drain it of its contents. But since the chalice continually renewed itself, by the time Lily had noticed what was going on Leyla had managed to drink several cups of the golden liquid. No one knew what the effects of over-ingesting the liquid of fire were. They only knew that the records of the Priesthood of the First mentioned that it should be drunk sparingly.

They had all been relieved when Leyla had not shown any signs of illness and not thought more of it until she turned three and her magicks suddenly began to manifest. Her level of power was off the charts, registering well over a level five which was the highest anyone had ever tested. So the group had agreed to hide this from everyone, and Lily and Kieran had been subduing Leyla's full powers for years.

Lily shook her head, "It is my fault."

"What matters now is to make sure we keep her powers under control for the time being," Aelwen said kindly. "Melia, do you know of any potions that might help?"

Melia nodded. "I have a power dampener recipe that might be worth a try if your spells aren't working anymore. You will have to find a way to give it to her without her realising though and it has quite a strong flavour."

"Thank you Melia," Kieran said gratefully. "We will figure out how to get her to take it without raising any questions."

"You might ask young Lara about that," Healer Thomas suggested. "She has quite the knack for potion-mixing. She even managed to make the Witchbane taste pleasant. Perhaps if you set it as a task in Potions class?" he asked Melia.

She nodded, "That's a great idea Healer Thomas."

"Speaking of Lara," Sofia's mom Sarra said, "what are we going to do about her? Deedee told me that her herb chamber recognised her true form."

Yelena's eyes widened with surprise. "How is that possible? The binding we worked on her when she was born should still be holding!"

Sarra shook her head sadly. "I am afraid it is wearing thin Yelena. If Deedee's chamber can see through the glamour then the King will be able to as well... you know he has the power of truthspeak."

"And he will be visiting the school next week," Daniel added.

They were all quiet while pondering the solution to this new problem. A problem they had not foreseen occurring so soon.

"What if we reworked the binding?" Melia asked. "If we all put our power into the spell it might hold just long enough for the King to finish his visit?"

"It is worth a try," Aelwen said. "And you and I can both try to limit Lara's exposure to the King at school—as long as she does not attract his attention in any way it should be enough." She turned to Yelena, her face betraying her worry. "But Yelena, if this does not work we will have to tell her—we cannot keep this a secret for much longer without putting her in greater danger."

Yelena nodded reluctantly.

***

Sunday morning Lara was woken by a small warm hand slipping into hers. She smiled with her eyes still closed as Talia burrowed against her under the covers.

"Good morning," Lara kissed Talia's forehead. "When did you get here?"

"I woke up last night and I was lonely," Talia looked at her with big brown eyes.

Lara chuckled. "Uh huh..."

"Well, I miss you when you're at school... I just wanted to sleep with you."

Lara hugged Talia against her chest tightly. "I'm just teasing you little bird, you know I like it when you snuggle into my bed."

Talia beamed at her and gave her a sloppy kiss. "C'mon, get up. I've been waiting for you to wake up for ages!! Yelena made pancakes!!"

She practically dragged Lara out of bed and down the stairs to the kitchen. Lara blinked in surprise as she took in the room. Balloons and streamers decked the walls and confetti was floating in the air. She noticed a huge pile of pancakes with candles on it. Yelena laughed at her surprised expression.

"Have you forgotten your own birthday sweet girl?"

Lara blinked. "It's my birthday? I completely forgot about it!"

"Happy birthday Lara!" Emmy and Sadie chimed as one, putting a haphazardly wrapped present in her hands. "It's from both of us," Emmy clarified.

"Open it!" Sadie said excitedly.

Talia helped Lara tear the paper off. Inside was a beautiful photo frame with a picture of all five of them in it.

"I made the photo frame," Sadie said proudly. "And Emmy decorated it!"

"It's beautiful," Lara hugged them. "I know just where to put this in my room at school!"

"Happy birthday sweet girl," Yelena said, handing her a small box.

Lara flipped the lid open and gasped. Nestled in a cushion of silk lay a beautiful and perfectly round moonstone the size of a walnut.

"Thanks Yelena! I love it!"

"Moonstones have a calming effect, I thought you could use it during your exams," Yelena smiled.

"My turn, my turn!!" Talia jumped up and down.

Lara took the small box from her hand and carefully unwrapped it. She smiled when she saw what it was. "A bubble charm bracelet! Did you make this yourself?" she asked Talia.

Talia nodded. "Yelena helped me with the spell but I made all the bubbles and the straps myself! I even used your favourite colour see!" she said pointing to the blue strap. "Now you can remember me every time you look at it!"

"I love it, thank you little bird!" Lara said, giving her a huge hug and putting her bracelet on. "But I don't need a bracelet to remind me of you, you're always on my mind."

Yelena turned away discreetly and wiped her eyes. She couldn't believe that Lara had just turned thirteen... she seemed so much older, more mature—she was practically like a mother to little Talia.

The door wards chimed and Yelena went to open it. Leyla, Sofia and Anna bustled in.

"Happy birthday!" Leyla squealed as she hugged Lara.

"Happy birthday!" Sofia and Anna squealed in unison.

Lara smiled with delight at having her friends there. "Thanks guys!" she said as she returned their hugs.

"Mmm, something smells good!" Leyla said, sneaking a peek at the pancake stack.

Anna laughed, "You and your stomach... where do you put it all!?"

"Hey!" Leyla grumbled good-naturedly, "I'm a growing girl!"

Everyone laughed at her comment as she was most undoubtedly the slimmest, most petite amongst the four of them.

They sat down to the birthday breakfast. The pancakes were strawberry and lemon, Lara's favourite. And there were fresh baked rolls and jam and chocolate cake too.

"Do you want to adopt me too?" Leyla asked Yelena. "My mom is great but she can't bake like you!"

Yelena chuckled. "I'll make you up a box to take home, how's that?"

"Thanks Yelena!" Leyla exclaimed. She turned to Lara, "Time for you to open your presents from us!"

She pulled a slim case out of her pocket and handed it to Lara. "This is from me, I hope you like it!"

Lara opened the case, inside was a beautiful miniature silver harp. "It's beautiful!" she exclaimed. "It will look amazing on my mantelpiece at school! Thank you!"

"It's not just an ornament!" Leyla declared. "Watch this!" She pressed the top of the harp and music flooded the room. "It plays a different tune each time!" she explained. "It senses your mood and picks the song you need to hear!"

"Wow! It's great!" Lara enthused.

"This is from me and Sofia," Anna said, handing Lara a large packet.

Lara smiled at her friends and hurriedly tore open the paper. It was an incense burner in the shape of a phoenix and a large selection of herbs and oils.

"We know how much you like herbs and things... we got it at Deedee's the other day after you left!" Sofia said.

"I love it!" Lara said, hugging her friends. "Thank you everyone, I love all my presents."

"I almost put my foot in it so many times!" Leyla confessed. "I kept almost blurting out your surprise birthday party!"

"Well, I really didn't have a clue!" Lara reassured her.

When they were done eating Yelena shooed them upstairs, telling them that she would clean up. They spent most of the day with Lara's sisters in her room chatting and playing games. No one had space for lunch after the huge breakfast, not even Leyla, although she did eat a couple of cookies that Yelena brought up to them. The day seemed to whizz past and the girls' parents came to get them all too soon.

"Bye!" Lara waved at Leyla who was the last to leave, "Thanks for everything!"

"See you tomorrow morning!" Leyla called out as she got into her mom's hovercar.

Lara watched her friend fly off as Lily cast the flyspell. Yelena came to stand behind her on the porch.

"Good day?" she asked putting an arm around Lara's shoulders.

"Great day!" Lara corrected, leaning into Yelena. "Thank you for organising it."

"My pleasure," Yelena's eyes sparkled. "You know some say thirteen is a magical number."

Lara yawned. "Well, I better get to bed, I have to be up early tomorrow morning."

"Of course," Yelena frowned slightly into Lara's hair. "It's a big day tomorrow with the King's visit."

She stayed sitting on the porch for a long time after Lara had gone to bed, lost in thought.

CHAPTER 12

"Do you see him?" Leyla whispered in Lara's ear as they all stood in lines in the main hall, waiting for the king.

Lara shook her head as she strained to see over the top of the head of the boy in front of her.

A loud gong sounded suddenly, reverberating through the stone laden chamber.

"That must be him arriving now!!" Leyla whispered loudly.

"Shh!" Jayla turned around and glared at them. "Show the King the respect he deserves and be quiet!" She turned to the girl next to her, "Seriously, how pathetic can you get... then again I suppose not everyone has grown up in the palace, practically a daughter to the King like I have."

Her tall blonde friend, a girl called Daria, nodded in agreement.

Leyla poked her tongue out at Jayla's back. "What a douche!" she said to Lara softly. "She thinks she's so much better than us... and Daria is even worse. I bet she doesn't even like Jayla, just hangs out with her because she thinks she's going to be queen one day!"

Lara stifled a giggle as Daria overheard Leyla and flushed bright red.

"Ladies and gentlemen, may I present King Merrick," a gruff voice echoed through the halls.

"Thank you Elder Jamal," a deep voice replied. "I am honoured to be visiting this fine institution today and I hope to meet as many of you as I can."

Lara caught her first glimpse of the King. She had seen pictures of him of course, but he looked younger and more relaxed in person. All three of his sons obviously took after him in looks although his eyes were green instead of brown. She watched as he greeted all the teachers one by one.

"He's different than what I expected," Leyla whispered.

Lara nodded, "I know what you mean... he seems so normal and relaxed."

King Merrick brushed his dark hair out of his eyes, the gesture reminding Lara of Xan. "Thank you so much for this warm welcome," he smiled. "I apologise if you have had to stand about all morning waiting on me... I'm sure you are all quite devastated to have missed your morning classes," he said eliciting a laugh from the crowd of students in the hall. "I'm not going to bore you all with a long speech, instead I thought I would let you get back to your classes. I will be coming around to all the different departments to see you at work." His eyes twinkled, "And, at the end of the day I will have a special announcement to make."

Everyone started clapping as the King walked out of the hall with Aelwen.

"I was expecting something... well something more," Leyla said disappointed.

"Do you wish there had been trumpets and red carpets and rose petals being scattered at the King's feet?" Lara teased.

Leyla grinned, "Well, it would have been a start... it was all just so 'normal.'" She looked at her watch. "Anyway, I better go. I'll see you at Potions next period ok?"

"See you then," Lara said as she headed towards the Healing Chamber.

Xan caught up with Lara in the hall leading to Healer Thomas's classroom.

"Hi Lara!" he said.

"Hi," she smiled at him.

He smiled at her shyly, "Happy birthday... Leyla mentioned it was your birthday yesterday."

"Thanks."

"I uh, got you something... it's not much, but I know how you like books... anyway... here, this is for you." He handed her a neatly wrapped rectangular present.

Lara opened it. It was a book on ancient herbology and healing, *A Million and One Ancient Cures.* She knew for a fact that it had been out of print for decades as she had looked everywhere for a copy. They had one in the school library but it was in the restricted section and could only be viewed there and not checked out. She looked up at him.

"Thank you Xan... it's a really thoughtful gift. I've been looking for this book for ages! How did you get it?"

"I overheard you asking Mrs Potts the librarian about it... I talked to my father's librarian Zarnac, he knows the best places to find old books... well he found it for me."

Lara touched the book's cover reverently. It was still in excellent condition. "Thank you so much."

He flushed slightly. "Anyway... we should head to class before Healer Thomas sends out a search party."

They were the last to arrive and hurriedly took their seats as Healer Thomas began to speak.

"Now, today we are going to explore an area of healing that is sorely underused." He waved his hand and pots of plants and herbs appeared on each student's table. They were blackening and shrivelled.

"What are we going to do with these?" Adam, one of the wolf-shifters asked as he sniffed the dying plants. "Surely we cannot make medicine from putrid plants?"

"You are absolutely right," their teacher said. "If you were to use these plants as they are you would probably do more harm than good. Most plants become toxic as they wither... a sort of defence mechanism if you will."

"So we could end up poisoning our patients?" a pretty fey called Libby asked.

Healer Thomas nodded. "Exactly. And that is why today's class is so important. We live in Lantis, a big and rich city, there is never a shortage of fresh supplies to be had. But if you join the Healer Corps then you might find you are sent to one of the more remote locations on Azmantium. Take the Kari desert for example. Many people still live there in tribes, following the ancient ways. Do you think you will find fresh plants and herbs growing there?" He shook his head. "There is a multitude of rich flora indigenous to the desert but there are also many that cannot survive the long hot days and the ice cold temperatures at night. How can a healer cure the ill without the necessary ingredients?" He looked around the class, only Lara's hand was up.

"Lara?"

"You improvise?" she said uncertainly.

He nodded, "Go on."

"Well," she thought for a minute, "you could try to create new potions and pomades from the plants that you do have access to... and doesn't the Kari desert have hot mud marshes that have healing properties? Maybe they could be used to boost the potency of the cures?"

Healer Thomas smiled. "Ah, an innovative mind... exactly what the healing profession is sorely lacking! Very good Lara!" He turned to the class. "One of the biggest problems in our profession today is that we have become complacent. Easy access to good quality herbs and potion making tools like burners and cauldrons, as well as text book teaching, has left many of our kind unable to perform when faced with a situation where the conditions are less than perfect."

He pointed to the drooping plants on the table. "Lara is right about using your imagination for healing. However, there is another option that can be used instead of, or as well as what she suggested."

He touched the leaf of the Jari plant on his desk. A soft golden glow emanated from his fingertips. The class watched raptly as the golden thread of magicks twined itself around the plant and it slowly straightened its bent spine, the black fading into a vibrant healthy blue. He removed his hand and showed them the plant. The golden glow lingered for a few seconds longer and then vanished.

"What I have just done is 'heal' the plant. Now it is safe to use this plant for potions. This technique can be invaluable in a situation where your resources are limited."

He flicked his fingers and the temperature in the chamber suddenly changed, becoming unbearably hot and dry.

"This is a simulation of desert conditions," Healer Thomas said, wiping a bead of sweat from his brow. "Observe the plant I just healed."

The entire class watched with interest as the Jari plant on his desk began to wither before their very eyes.

"As you can see many plants are highly sensitive to climactic elements. The Jari is a particularly temperature sensitive plant. It also doesn't thrive in dry conditions, preferring a moister atmosphere."

"So how can you use these plants in those locations if they cannot even withstand a few minutes there?" Libby asked.

"Ah, now we get to the point of today's lesson," Healer Thomas smiled. "What we are going to learn today is how to preserve herbs and plants and how to 'resuscitate' them." He touched the plant again and the magicks flowed through his fingers returning the Jari to its former glory.

"Cool!" Adam said.

Thomas's eyes sparkled. "I'm glad you approve Adam." He pointed at the plants on their tables. "Now, I want you to pair up with a partner and take turns trying to 'heal' the plants. I warn you though, it is not as easy as it looks and requires much more finesse than when dealing with people. Plants are more delicate in essence and the amount and flow of power you send to them should be tempered accordingly."

Lara turned to Xan, who was sitting next to her.

"Do you want to go first?" she asked.

"Sure," he shrugged.

He pulled a sickly skeletal plant in front of himself and focussed hard on it. He touched it and sent out his power. It seemed to swell a little but then returned to its previous sorry state. He tried a few more times but couldn't get the plant to do much more than grow a little, and only temporarily.

"It really isn't as easy as it looks!" he exclaimed.

Lara looked around the class. No one else seemed to be having any luck either.

"Time to let your partners have a try!" Healer Thomas called out a few minutes later.

Xan gently pushed the Luxus plant in front of Lara. She looked at the spiky plant. It looked as though it had shrivelled beyond repair. She touched a finger gently to the tip of a thorn and closed her eyes. She felt a weak hum from the plant as if it were asking for her help. She carefully pulled on her magicks and very gently allowed it to coil out of her and around the Luxus. The hum beneath her fingers grew louder as she continued to feed the plant with her magic.

"Lara! You've done it!" Xan exclaimed.

Lara opened her eyes without removing her hand from the plant. The Luxus had grown a foot in height and was no longer black but a vivid orange colour with deep crimson thorns. It hummed loudly now as if in thanks.

"Well done Lara!" her teacher said excitedly.

Everyone turned to stare at her. No one else had managed to revive their plants.

"That's amazing!" Libby said to Lara. "How do you do it?"

"I don't know," Lara said, puzzled that she was the only one that had managed it.

"You obviously have an affinity for plants," Healer Thomas chuckled, "as well as very advanced control of your magicks." A huge smile lit up his face. "Now, don't be discouraged," he said to the rest of the class. "This is normally something that takes even my best students weeks to perfect. You will all be able to do it by the end of the term. Once you have managed this then we will work on performing the spell in various different climactic conditions."

Adam groaned. "Seriously?! We can't even do it under normal conditions!"

The teacher chuckled, "You will all get there, I promise!"

The gong sounded, indicating the end of the lesson.

"Lara could you wait a minute?" Healer Thomas asked as her fellow students all filed out to head to their various classes.

Lara nodded. Healer Thomas waited until the last student had left and then waved his hand over the chamber, sound-proofing the room.

"Can I help you clear up?" she asked.

"That would be very good of you," he said. "But before you do, can you do something for me?"

"Of course," she said. "What would you like me to do?"

He placed a charred black twig with hundreds of tiny sharp thorns in front of her.

"This is a Nexar plant," he explained. "Can you revive it for me so I can see how you do it?"

Lara reached out to the plant.

"I would like you to talk me through each step of your process," he said.

She touched the plant and closed her eyes. The hum from its essence was so weak it was barely there.

"I am feeling its hum... it is dying, almost weakened beyond repair... it's asking for help..." she trailed off. "I'm going to send my magicks to it now."

She unleashed a gentle but steady stream of magicks on the Nexar and listened as the hum grew louder as it had with the Luxus plant. She opened her eyes to find a small, but very healthy looking purple plant with hundreds of tiny fluorescent yellow thorns. She looked at Healer Thomas. He was watching with an odd look on his face.

"You said it hummed?" he asked.

Lara nodded, "Yes, but I couldn't hear it... I don't know if it makes any sense, but I felt it through my fingertips—as if the plant were communicating with me... does that sound silly?" she asked anxiously.

"Not at all," Thomas said a thoughtful look on his face. "I will admit that I have never felt any such thing myself... but that is not to say that it does not exist."

Lara pulled her hands off of the Nexar and one of the small thorns pierced her skin. Both she and Healer Thomas watched in shock as the plant tripled in size and began to glow.

"Let me see your hand!" Healer Thomas exclaimed, examining her hand.

A tiny droplet of blood was visible on her index finger where the thorn had broken skin. He paled and quickly healed her cut with his magicks.

"It's ok, I just poked myself on the thorn," Lara said, surprised by his reaction.

"Of course my dear... listen why don't you head to your next class? I can tidy up in here."

"Are you sure?" she asked.

"Yes, yes, run along, I'm sure Melia is wondering where you are. Just tell her you were helping me."

Lara nodded.

"Lara?" he called out as she was about to leave.

She turned back to look at him.

"Let's not mention this to anyone for now... you are already so far ahead of the rest, I wouldn't want them to feel pressured by your abilities."

Lara smiled. "Of course, Healer Thomas."

Thomas waited until he was alone and then slumped in his chair. This was not good, not good at all. He shivered as he looked at the giant plant in front of him. Nexar never grew beyond eight or nine inches... this one was almost a foot tall, and it was still glowing with a soft silver hue. How was he going to tell Yelena about this? He was more than impressed with Lara's control over her magicks, a control that was sorely necessary in her case. And he was in awe of her raw natural talent with herbs and healing. But this... this was something else... something forbidden... it wasn't until her blood fell on the Nexar that it made its transformation into a giant version of itself. There was only one possible explanation for it... Lara had blood magicks. This changed everything.

CHAPTER 13

Later that night Lara slept restlessly. Strange dreams and images invaded her sleep, making her toss and turn until she came to the vivid fields where she'd met Asena in her last dream.

She walked quickly through the flower-laden meadows and back across the stream to the opening of the cave. Asena was waiting for her just as she had known she would be.

"Welcome back," the beautiful young woman said, embracing her. "I have been waiting for you to visit."

Lara felt a sudden peace settle over her like a comforting blanket.

"I'm sorry I haven't been back sooner... life has been pretty hectic lately."

Asena nodded. "It was not a reproach dear one... I know you have much on your mind. I felt your worry today."

Lara pulled back startled. "You felt me?"

Asena led Lara to a comfy armchair by the fire. "I can always sense you dear one... and I felt what happened today."

"What did happen today?" Lara asked. "Healer Thomas was very strange about the whole thing... did I do something wrong?"

"No, of course not dear child," Asena said. "I believe your teacher is finding it hard to come to terms with your many talents... I do not think he has ever had such a pupil before. And the speed your powers are growing at are making him slightly nervous, especially with the King being at magic school this week."

"Why does the King make him nervous?" Lara said puzzled.

"He is worried that you will attract the King's attention," Asena answered.

"Not that I want to attract anyone's attention... but why is that such a bad thing?"

"The King likes to surround himself with special people Lara, especially those with strong and rare powers..."

"What do you mean?" Lara asked.

"Just that he wants the best and brightest of Azmantium on his elite forces," Asena said vaguely.

Lara shrugged, "Most of my friends' parents work for the King directly, as does aunt Aelwen... they seem to like their jobs."

Asena bowed her golden head for a moment, choosing her words with care. "They do what they do for the people of Azmantium Lara. They are in service to the people. The King is just one man... remember that in the days to come," she said cryptically.

"Asena, what exactly did I do to the Nexar?"

Asena looked at her closely for a moment and then nodded as if she had made a decision. "It was not anything you did per say... it was your blood that affected the Nexar in that manner"

"My blood?"

"Yes," Asena walked over to the fire and stared at the flickering blue flames. "A long time ago there was an ability called blood magicks. Have you ever heard of it?"

Lara shook her head.

"It was rare even then... an ability which few had and many wanted." She turned to Lara, "Many people lost their way due to the power that the blood magicks gave them... the ones that had it sought to take control, the ones that did not have it sought to eradicate all beings who possessed it. Some say it was the root of the problem—that it was what caused the beginning of the Great War."

Lara frowned, "Does that mean I am going to do bad things?"

Asena smiled and shook her head. "We each follow the path of our choice in life Lara. Never let anyone convince you otherwise. Besides, not all blood magic users were power hungry and bad. There were many who sought to use their ability for good—to help others, to heal..." She sat next to Lara on the sofa. "The problem with blood magic Lara is that there are those who would try to control you to control your power even if you do not wish to use it for personal gain ..." she trailed off. "The other drawback is that blood magic has been forbidden for centuries. This is why Healer Thomas was so nervous when he saw what you could do."

"What about all the other blood magic users?" Lara asked.

"There aren't any Lara; you are the first to be born with it in a long time."

"What do you mean it's forbidden?"

Asena looked at her intently. "Lara, dear child, you cannot let anyone find out about the blood magic outside of those you trust implicitly."

"*What would happen if I got found out?*" *Lara said worriedly.*

"*You would be in grave danger... I tell you too much when I say all of this, but the situation leaves me no other choice. It would be too dangerous to allow you to remain in the dark about your powers,*" *she muttered, as if to herself.*

"*There is more you are not telling me, isn't there?*" *Lara asked.*

Asena nodded. "*Telling you is not my place Lara... that must come from another, although I sense that you will not have to wait long before your questions are answered.*"

"*I have so many questions!*" *Lara exclaimed.*

"*I know dear child, but now is not the time... you already have enough on your young shoulders with this new secret you must keep.*"

Lara nodded with acceptance.

"*I know that you are impatient to find out more,*" *Asena said.* "*I am happy and proud that you can have the strength to wait... I do not think most children your age would be so mature about it.*"

"*Can you at least tell me something more about yourself?*" *Lara asked.*

Asena's eyes sparkled. "*You and I have much in common, although I don't share your depth of passion for healing quite in the same way.*"

"*Why do you live here? And where is here?*" *Lara asked, looking around the cave.*

"*I don't 'live' here exactly... you could say that this is a manifestation of your own imagination.*"

Lara looked at her intently. "Am I imagining you as well, or are you real?"

Asena sighed, "Lara, I want to answer your questions honestly but to do so I would have to break an oath I made long ago... all I can tell you is that I am real, just not in the way you are thinking." She froze suddenly and looked at Lara, "Hurry Lara, you have to go back, you have to go back right away!"

"What is it?"

"I sense a dark presence approaching Lara, they must not find you here with me... quickly, and you must go back across the stream as fast as you can!" She rushed towards Lara, gave her a brief hug and ushered her out of the cave.

"Will I be able to come back?" Lara asked before she left.

Asena nodded, "Now go, quickly... and tell no one about our meeting."

***

Lara woke up in her own bed again. This time she wasn't as disorientated. Leyla bounded into her room just as she had finished getting dressed.

"Oh good, you're almost ready! Lara!! I just heard! The King would like us all to meet in the main hall. He has an important announcement to make!"

"Good morning to you too!" Lara teased, trying to shake off the deep feeling of unease that Asena's words had triggered.

Leyla grinned at her sheepishly. "Sorry! I'm just so excited!! I wonder what it's all about. Do you think that the King is going to announce his heir already?"

Lara shook her head, "I don't know... and remember Leyla, we are not supposed to know about the 'heir' issue, unless you want to advertise the fact that we have been traipsing around the school at night and eavesdropping to boot!"

"Oh yeah, you're right! Don't worry my lips are sealed... now c'mon!" she said, practically dragging Lara from the room.

The main hall was already packed when they got there, hundreds of voices chattering loudly as everyone wondered the purpose for the summons.

"Why do you suppose we're here?" Max asked Lara as he came to stand beside her.

"I don't know, maybe Xan will know."

"I haven't seen him or his brothers since last night," Max said. "I don't think they were in their rooms either. They must have gone to stay with their father in the royal wing of the school."

"There's a royal wing?" Lara asked in astonishment, she hadn't ever come across it. She wondered if Anna and Sofia knew about it.

Max laughed at the expression on her face. "Yeah, it's on the east side of the building, you know, the one with the big turret. It's sealed off by powerful magicks though, and only the royal family and the Elders know how to unspell the wards around it." He smiled, "No one knows exactly where the entrance is except for them."

"How do you know all this?" Leyla asked Max with interest.

"I used to be good friends with Darren. He wasn't always like he is today. He actually used to be quite nice. He told me about it once."

Silence fell across the hall suddenly as the large solid door swung open dramatically and the King came in accompanied by his usual small retinue of elite guards and Elders Aelwen and Jamal.

"Move it losers!" Jayla elbowed Lara hard in the ribs as she pushed past to get to the front.

"Hey!" Leyla exclaimed. "We were here first!"

Jayla gave her a scathing look. "Is that Elder standing at the King's right hand your father?" she asked snidely. "I didn't think so... the King will be expecting to see me in the front row... as for you, I'm sure he couldn't care less—you're a nobody!"

Lara grabbed Leyla's arm and pulled her back. "Just let her go, she's not worth the trouble."

"I know," Leyla muttered, "but I would love to see her get what she deserves... she makes me so mad!"

"Good morning students," Aelwen's clear voice rang through the hall. "King Merrick requested we all gather here today as he has an important announcement to make." She moved away letting the King take centre stage.

"Good morning," the King beamed. "Once again I have to apologise for gathering you all here, especially at this time in the morning! I promise to be brief and let you get to your breakfasts." He paused and looked around the hall at the students. "As you might already know, it is customary for the King to elect an heir apparent once he has been in power for two hundred years... well, in a month's time I will have been King for two centuries. The time for me to announce my successor is fast approaching..."

A low murmuring started amongst the crowd.

"Who do you think he's chosen?"

"Oh, Seth of course... everyone knows that!"

"Well, why make such a big deal of announcing it then?"

King Merrick waited for the whispers to die down before he continued. "According to tradition, the King must choose his heir based on a number of qualities—strength, integrity, honour and wisdom." He gestured to someone and his three sons came to stand next to him. "Now, I know that you all expect me to announce my heir today... however, I have decided to delay my decision for a month. During that month I will be evaluating the progress of each contender. I mean to do that by means of a Karnac."

The student body began to whisper furiously at this news.

"Most of you probably don't know about the Karnac as it has not been used in some time... indeed not even in my long lifetime. It is an ancient custom which was used to ensure the rule of the best candidate."

"What's a Karnac?" Leyla whispered to Lara.

"I have no idea," she frowned.

"The Karnac is not as scary as it sounds," the King continued. "And before this gentleman in the front row ignites any panic-worthy rumours I can safely say that it does not involve a fight to the death," he grinned at the red-faced boy who had made the comment. "The Karnac is merely a competition, a sort of tournament if you will, which will test the mettle of our potential heirs through a series of challenges." He paused, his eyes twinkling. "This competition is about more than mere strength or magicks... it will test every aspect of the King to be."

He pulled out a long sword. It was tarnished silver with black diamonds encrusted in the handle. "This is Kai-Kohan, which in the language of our ancient fey ancestors, means King-maker. It is the sword of the Kings of our line and will only 'perform' for its true owner... it, not I, shall be choosing your future King."

Seth scowled darkly at his father. He was supposed to be King, not his two younger and weaker brothers. He had been in training all his life for that. He fumed silently as his father continued.

"You might wonder why I have not just chosen my own heir—why I am leaving the decision to Kai-Kohan..." he glanced at his sons. Seth seemed furious, Darren looked hopeful and Xan, well, Xan looked shell-shocked. "No King in over five centuries has had more than one son... I have three. I believe this to be the fairest way to find the next King. This way the people will know that the most worthy has been chosen by the most respected and ancient of magicks and not just by me."

He sheathed Kai-Kohan once more.

"Each competitor will need to choose a team of eight 'helpers.'" He turned to his sons and told them, "You must choose your team wisely as you will be very dependent on their aid to win these challenges. Your teams will be participating directly in the challenges alongside you. They may help with strategies, planning, research... everything except for the final challenge. Choose wisely, and remember to use their strengths to your advantage."

He turned back to the student body. "No one is obligated to compete, and if any of you are chosen as a team member you may decline. Although, as an added incentive to participate, I should probably mention that those who take part will be rewarded whether their team wins or loses."

"Gods!" exclaimed Leyla. "This is just too cool!! Do you think Xan will pick us? I would love to take part!"

Lara frowned as she looked at Xan. He didn't seem too excited about any of this. In fact, he looked quite upset. "I don't know that he really wants to be doing this," she said.

Leyla snorted, "Well, I don't think he has a choice really... besides, do you really think either Seth or Darren would make good kings?"

Lara shook her head at the thought of either of those two, known for their selfishness and rudeness to others, ruling their world one day. Leyla saw the expression on her face. "Yeah, I didn't think so."

"Well, if he picks us," Sofia said joining them, "we will do our best to help him win!"

"Yes, we will," Anna said as she high-fived Sofia.

"The Karnac will begin next term," the King continued. "The last challenge will be on the day before the end of the next term, following which the Kai-Kohan will make its choice." He turned to his sons, "I urge you to begin assembling your teams and making preparations for the challenges. No one will know the nature of the challenges until the morning they take place although you can be sure that the major areas of magicks will be tested in some way or another. Elder Aelwen will give out the necessary information concerning the Karnac to all participants once they have been selected." He smiled at the students, "I should probably also mention that Elder Aelwen has decided to cancel all exams this term and the next so that we can all focus on the preparations for the Karnac!"

His announcement met with loud cheers from the students. The hall buzzed with chatter as the King left the room. Everyone was in great spirits, excited about the news... everyone that is except Seth and Xan.

.

CHAPTER 14

That afternoon Lara sat in her comfy armchair reading. Leyla had gone off with Anna and Sofia and some other kids to the rec room. They were all really excited about the upcoming Karnac. A knock sounded at the door.

"The door is open!" she called.

Xan opened the door. "Hi Lara, am I disturbing you?"

"No," she smiled, setting her book down, "come in. I was just reading the book you got me."

He looked at the thick hard cover book. "Wow!" he exclaimed, seeing where her bookmark was. "Have you already read all of that?!"

She nodded enthusiastically. "It's a great book! It's got so many healing tricks and concoctions in it that aren't in the medical text books we use here!"

"I'm glad you like it so much," he smiled.

"Do you want a drink?" she asked him.

"Sure."

Lara waved her hand and two Zay berry juices came floating out of the cool box.

Xan took a sip. "This is delicious, what's in it?"

·"I was experimenting and mixed Zay berries with Mali essence... it tastes great and is great for energy too."

He took another sip, looking thoughtful.

"What is it?" she asked him.

He looked up at her. "I was wondering... and you can say no, I really would understand... but do you think you might want to be on my team for the Karnac?"

Lara smiled, "Of course, although I'm not sure if you shouldn't choose someone older, with more magicks experience?"

He shook his head and handed her a thin booklet. "These are the rules and procedures about the Karnac. Elder Aelwen gave them to us after my father left."

Lara read the booklet quickly.

"As you can see in section B, it mentions the rules concerning team-building. Every team must have a healer..." He looked at Lara, "You are honestly, by far, the best healer I know. It doesn't matter that you are the newest and youngest in the class... none of us can even come close to your level of medical understanding."

Lara smiled, "If you're sure, then count me in."

Xan looked relieved.

"So, who else do you need on your team?"

He looked at the booklet. "I need a protector, an illusionist, an elemental, a shifter—it doesn't say what kind, so I guess it doesn't matter, and a fey. If we count you as the healer, that makes six. The remaining two can be chosen freely with no conditions attached." He sighed, "I have no idea who to choose."

"Well, Leyla is a very talented elemental," Lara said. "She has a very strong tie to the earth. Anna is a protector and Sofia is an illusionist, they are all very good at what they do... although you don't have to choose them just because they are my friends," she added.

"No, that's great!" He exclaimed. "Do you mind helping me set up the team? I could really use your help. I don't just want people that are strong and have powerful magicks... I want a team that likes each other and works well together."

"Okay!" Lara said excitedly. "How about Max and Adam? They are both shifters but Adam is a healer and Max is an elemental, and he's a whiz with air magic."

He nodded. "And Libby? Healing is her second weaker power, she is actually fey and really good at glamours. And maybe Nat? He's also a protector and I've seen his wards and runes, he's really good."

"Great! So that's eight already."

"Phew," Xan slouched in his chair. "Thanks for the help... I was dreading finding a team."

"You didn't look too excited about the whole Karnac thing," Lara said.

"Not really... it's just that I always thought Seth was dad's heir... I never wanted to be King, I still don't."

Lara looked at him intently. "But maybe that's exactly why you would make a great one in the future."

He looked at her puzzled.

"Well, you are obviously not power hungry or self-centred if you don't even want to rule Azmantium... most people would give their right arm to be King, and live in a palace and make all the decisions... the fact that that doesn't appeal to you means that if you became King it would be for the right reasons, such as wanting to help others and maintaining a safe and happy world for us all to live in."

"Sounds like you deserve to be King more than any of us," he joked.

She shook her head. "I wouldn't want that! I wouldn't have any time to see my patients!"

He laughed heartily. "You must be the only person I know who would rather become a Healer than a Queen!"

"Takes one to know one," she retorted.

He grinned as he stood up. "Well, I'd better go and find the names on our list and see if they all agree to join my team."

"I am sure they will," Lara said.

"Thanks again for helping me figure it all out," he said before closing the door.

***

"This is so exciting!" Leyla whispered later that night as they crept out of their room.

"I know! I can't wait to see what we find on the other side of the secret door!" Anna enthused.

"Not that!" Leyla said. "Although I'm excited about that too. I was talking about us all being on Xan's team for the Karnac!"

"My mom was so excited to hear that we were chosen to take part!" Sofia said. "She promised she will help us as much as she can during the holidays to get us ready."

"Tam said that there is to be a big ball given at the end of next term to mark the end of the Karnac and to celebrate the choosing of the heir!" Anna said. "I can't wait!"

"Do you have the opener spell?" Lara asked Sofia as they tiptoed down the dark stairway.

"It's right here," she said, patting her pocket.

They crossed the large hall slowly, careful to not make any noise. Leyla lifted the tapestry covering the hidden doorway and Sofia took out the flat silver disc which contained the spell. She carefully placed it onto the door and then stepped back. They waited as golden runes flowed out of the disc and swirled around the door in a complex dance. They all held their breaths as they heard a click and the door slowly swung open.

"Oh my Gods!" Anna whispered, "I can't believe we did it!"

"Of course we did!" Sofia snorted. "Deedee gave us that spell... when have you ever known her spells not to work?"

"Shh, come on, let's go in and check it out!" Leyla said.

They carefully walked in, taken aback as the dark corridor on the other side lit up suddenly.

"Oh no!" Sofia said, "It's motion-activated!"

They stood there for a while, not daring to move... but no one came to tell them off.

"It's probably just a light for when people use it," Lara said. She waved her fingers and the lights dimmed until they were almost out. "There, this way we can see and explore without attracting too much attention."

The walls were of solid Roxan wood, a beautiful mahogany-hued colour. An odd choice for a secret passageway only few would ever get to see. They continued down the long tunnel-like corridor until they reached a sort of ante-chamber.

"Where to now?" Leyla asked, as they looked at the four different doors in the room.

"Let's try this one!" Sofia said, pushing open the first door on the right.

It led through to a dark and draughty tunnel. A myriad of silvery spider webs glinted softly in the dim glow of the torch she was holding.

"Ew, yuck!" Anna exclaimed, backing up until she was almost standing on top of Leyla.

"Anna is scared of spiders," Sofia said, brushing past some webs.

"I'm not scared!" Anna clarified. "I just don't like them!"

She inched her way into the tunnel, carefully avoiding the webs as though they were deadly. Lara and Leyla followed close behind.

"I wonder where this leads to," Sofia mused after they had been walking for a few minutes.

"It's a huge building... could be anywhere," Leyla replied.

They finally reached yet another door. Thankfully it was unlocked as they had already used up the opener spell on the first door. Sofia pushed it open cautiously. The girls looked at each other in confusion. It was just a small chamber made of stone. There was no furniture, no other doors... nothing.

"That's disappointing," Sofia huffed. "Why have a huge long tunnel leading all the way here just for this?"

They were just about to leave and go back when they heard the voices.

"Do you have everything you need?" It was Aelwen's.

"Yes, thank you... you have been very kind to me," a voice answered her.

"Where are the voices coming from?" Leyla whispered.

Lara held the torch along the walls and then the ground. There were tiny vents in the floorboards. She pointed to the vents.

"Look, that's where they are coming from, Aelwen must be below us."

"Not at all my dear, it was the least we could do... I'm just sorry we weren't able to get you out sooner. If we had only known you were still alive..." Aelwen trailed off.

"You couldn't have known Aelwen," the other voice said calmly. "Even my own mother thought me dead... the body they showed her as proof even tricked her. Whoever performed that illusion must be powerful indeed. You came for me as soon as you heard, that's all that matters... I owe you my life."

"If that young guard hadn't been one of our own…"

"That is not important anymore," the voice said. "You know what matters now. I have contacted the other Oracles, I have shown them what I have seen through a memory-link… they will stand with us when the time comes."

"Are you sure you want to stay here? We can arrange for the other Oracles to get you very discreetly."

"Thank you but no, there is much I need to do, and I need to be here… it is part of my destiny. She will need my help in the days to come, especially if we are to conceal her from Ragnar." Her voice trembled on the name belying her otherwise calm tone.

"Very well," Aelwen replied. "It is a big sacrifice you are making for us… I cannot tell you how invaluable your help is."

"Your essence is bright Elder Aelwen. You are walking the path of light—that is all I need to know to offer my help."

"Who was Aelwen talking to?" Sofia whispered once Aelwen left and the voices stopped.

"I don't know," Lara said, puzzled. "The voices were too muffled by the stone walls. I only recognised Aelwen's because I'm so familiar with it. Although there was something about that other voice…" she trailed off.

"This is brilliant!" Leyla enthused. "It's just like in my fantasy books!"

"They mentioned the Oracles," Anna said gravely. "There are supposedly only a small number left on Azmantium, and no one knows where they are."

"How come?" Lara asked.

"My mom told me that Oracles have very strong magicks and that they can see the threads of the future…

but that if they use their powers too often they can go mad," Sofia said.

"They are also hyper-sensitive to the feelings of those around them as they are natural empaths. I guess it's hard being around people and feeling everything they feel."

Lara nodded, "It must be some sensory overload."

"I think that's why they live away from others... that, and because there are many people who would like to get their hands on an Oracle for the power of foresight."

Something clicked in Lara's mind as she remembered Elina's memories. Elina was an Oracle, and she had been taken for her powers. The woman Aelwen was talking to had to be Elina. She thought about telling the others, but then realised that she couldn't tell them how she knew without betraying Elina's secret, and potentially putting her in danger.

"Let's go," Sofia said after they had waited a few more minutes. "She must be alone now, there are no voices."

"Yeah! Let's check out some of the other tunnels!" Leyla said excitedly.

They made their way back to the first room with the four doors.

"How about we search them in order?" Sofia said, opening the door next to the one they had come back from.

The girls nodded and followed her in. They stared in awe at the tunnel they had entered. The walls were cave-like with gleaming silver crystals growing on the walls and ceiling.

"What is this place?" Leyla breathed reverently.

"And what are those crystals? I've never seen anything like it, not even in Deedee's shop!" Sofia exclaimed.

Lara touched a finger to the tip of a crystal. It seemed to pulse under her skin. A soft glow began to resonate through the corridor, lighting up their way.

They walked until they reached a door at the end. It led to a large circular chamber made entirely of white crystal, except for the large violet crystal embedded on a pedestal in the centre of the room.

"Wow!" Leyla breathed. "What is this place?"

They walked around the room wordlessly—the white crystals lighting up softly as they passed them. Lara walked up to the centre pedestal, drawn to the violet crystal by some unknown force. She gingerly reached out a hand and touched the cool smooth facets of the stone.

"Lara!" Sofia exclaimed as the entire chamber was flooded with beams of purple light.

Leyla, Sofia and Anna watched, frozen like statues as the centre circle where the pedestal was lifted slowly into the air, taking Lara with it.

Lara held onto the crystal with both hands now, oblivious to what was going on around her. She didn't notice the dancing lights, nor did she even realise she was hovering six feet in the air. She stared at the crystal as though hypnotised.

She was no longer in the secret passageways at school, but in a small clearing in the forest.

"So, we meet again young friend," a soft voice spoke to her. It was Caliana, the lady from her registration test. "I was not

expecting to see you again so soon child." She walked towards Lara and laid an arm on her shoulder. "I fear that by coming here you have set in motion events which cannot be stalled any longer."

Lara looked at her quizzically.

Caliana sighed, her green eyes filled with worry. "I will help you as much as I am able to child, yet it is a long and hard road you walk."

She pulled away from Lara a little and brought her hands together. The earth beneath their feet began to vibrate and shake. Lara held on to a tree next to her as she watched a large crevice split the earth apart. Caliana raised her arms to the skies and as she did a silver staff rose from inside the earth. The tiny violet stones in its tip glinted in the light of the red suns as it first rose and then hovered over to Lara. The earth sealed itself back together once more as if nothing had just happened.

Caliana walked back over to Lara, "Take it child, it is yours by right."

Lara held out her hand and the staff settled into her palm. "What is it for?" she asked Caliana.

"It is your destiny," Caliana replied gravely. "And now you must leave this place... I fear that they may track the scent of powers back to us. Leave, hide the staff and do not tell any of whence it came."

***

Lara opened her eyes as the pedestal settled back on the chamber floor. She looked at her friends, who were staring at the staff in her hand with shock.

CHAPTER 15

Leyla took a step towards Lara and then stopped suddenly as Lara began to glow, her skin turning a dark pearly silver hue.

"Lara?!" she exclaimed.

Anna and Sofia stood behind Leyla, mouths wide open in shock.

"What's happening?" Leyla asked frantically as Lara's pupils began to elongate into black cat-like slits and her usually deep blue eyes turned an almost translucent golden colour.

"I don't know!" Sofia gasped. "She touched the purple crystal... hovered in the air for a few seconds and then this!"

"A few seconds?" Lara asked surprised. "But I thought I was gone longer..."

"Gone? Gone where?" Anna clamoured. "You were here the whole time!"

Lara looked down at her arms, they were shimmering. She blinked her eyes a few times, her vision had become strange—colours were more vibrant like when she visited Asena in the dream world.

"Oh my Gods!" Anna breathed. "What are we going to do? I don't think your concealment charm is going to be able to hide this! What should we do?"

Sofia shook her head. "I don't know... I don't know what's causing this. Oh, I wish Deedee were here, she would know what to do!"

The girls were so busy trying to think of a solution that they didn't notice what was happening to Lara at first. She crumpled to the floor as her entire body bowed and spasmed out of control.

"Lara!" Leyla rushed over to her when she saw her friend in trouble. "What's happening?"

Lara writhed in silence, the glow around her body getting brighter and brighter until Leyla could no longer look at her directly. She turned to Anna and Sofia.

"We have to go get Aunt Aelwen, she will know what to do!"

"I'll go!" Sofia volunteered.

None of them gave any thought to the trouble they might be in as they sought to help their friend. Sofia was about to leave to fetch Aelwen when the door swung open. The girls held their breaths as a pretty young woman with silver eyes strode in with purpose and walked straight to where Lara was convulsing, followed closely by Aelwen.

"You were right!" Aelwen said to the young woman that none of them recognised. "I am sorry if you thought I doubted you... I just couldn't see how she would find this chamber..." She crouched over Lara and grasped her hands—a steady stream of blue magicks passing from her to Lara as she chanted something under her breath. When she was finished and Lara had quietened somewhat she looked at the three frightened girls, huddled in a corner. "I should have suspected you three would be involved!" she said kindly.

"It's all my fault!" Sofia burst out. "It was my idea to look for the secret passageways... we just wanted an adventure Elder Aelwen. We never realised it would be dangerous or that Lara would get hurt!"

Aelwen stood and walked over to the girls while the young woman sat on the floor, cradling Lara's head on her lap so she didn't hurt herself with the slight tremors still racking her body.

"Lara is going to be just fine," she reassured them. "Believe it or not, she isn't in any pain."

Leyla looked at Lara who was still twitching.

"I promise you," Aelwen repeated, "she is fine."

The girls watched in horror as Lara's whole body went up in blue flames.

"Elder Aelwen, she's on fire! Why aren't you doing something?" Leyla asked dubiously.

It was the pretty young woman who answered. "She is becoming what she has always been." She looked at Aelwen, "There is no amount of magicks that can subdue the transformation for long at this point Elder Aelwen. You have done what you can, and it will hold for now but Lara has become too strong and the Tallan has come to her. No spells will bind her now." She shook her head, "There is no going back now Elder, the threads of destiny have been woven... the outcome will depend on her now, and her ability to control her powers."

"I feared as much... thank you Elina."

"I came as soon as I could!" Yelena ran in out of breath. She took in the scene before her. Leyla, Anna and Sofia were watching Lara, terror in their eyes. She ran to Lara and sat down next to her without touching her.

"Yelena, Lara is burning, why aren't you helping her?" Sofia asked shakily.

"We cannot stop what is happening Sofia... and see she is not burning."

Sure enough despite the flames flickering all over her, Lara did not seem to feel the heat.

Lara's golden slitted eyes shot open suddenly and she stared intensely into Elina's eyes. Elina tried to shield her mind as Lara began to pull on her thoughts and memories but Lara was too strong. Hundreds of images, fragmented memories from Elina's past flashed through her mind. Dark images, dungeons... heartbreak and sorrow... Lara tried desperately to pull back but something was keeping her locked on Elina's mind.

"Let go," Elina said calmly, despite the sweat pearling on her brow from the exertion of using her mental shield. "Lara, it is alright to let go... you are safe, amongst friends..."

Elina's soothing calmed the fire burning in Lara's stomach and slowly the fear receded and with it the memory-link broke. Elina slumped over, exhausted as Lara slowly stood up.

"I am so sorry!" she exclaimed, horrified at the breach of Elina's mind.

Elina smiled weakly. "It was an instinctive reaction Lara, a defence mechanism... You didn't do it on purpose."

Elina's silver eyes began to swirl like clouds of mercury. She stood up and stepped away from Lara. She spoke in a voice unlike her own, the deep tones echoing across the room.

"The child of the fire is born tonight, the earth is once more renewed. The skies are singing a joyful tune, the winds howling their welcoming sound. Born of fire and earth dragon-born comes to bring bright into the dark. She alone can light the way." An unseen wind lifted Elina's hair as her eyes flashed. *"Dark and long the path is where she must surely tread. Danger thorns the winding road to where this all must end."*

She turned to Lara suddenly and grabbed her hands, looking deeply into her eyes. *"Hope of all you are child, in you we must place our trust. In order to reset the balance of the earth you must start at the end, and end at the start."*

"What was that?!" Leyla said loudly.

Aelwen turned to her, "What you just saw my dear is something very few have been fortunate enough to witness—that was an Oracle in a prophecy trance."

"Cool!" Sofia piped up. "I didn't know Oracles still existed!"

"What did it mean?" Anna asked.

"Prophecies tend to be vague," Aelwen explained. "Their meaning often only becoming clear once events have taken place."

"What's the use in that?" Leyla asked, and then blushed furiously as she realised what she had just said.

"Sorry, I didn't mean it like that," she said to Elina sheepishly.

Elina smiled at her. "No offense taken. I have often wondered the use of prophecy myself."

Aelwen shook her head, "It gives us a place to start, a warning of what is to come… no one can see the future exactly—everything is always in a state of flux dependent on choices we all make every second of the day."

She turned to Lara, who was still glowing bright, flames dancing around her body. The staff Elina had called Tallan began to glow, the violet crystals on the end sending out purple flames which shot out of the tip and swirled around Lara, sealing her in a cage of light. Lara's entire body began to convulse as her body absorbed the purple light. She tried to let go of it but it held fast, as though glued to her hand. She fell back as liquid fire coursed through her veins setting her nerve endings alight with magicks. She lifted her hand and gasped when she saw that claws had grown out of her fingers. Large talon-like claws. She crashed onto the floor as another spasm hit her. Leyla fell to her knees next to Lara in horror when she caught sight of Lara writhing on the floor.

"Yelena!" Lara rasped, turning her head towards her foster mother. "What's happening to me?"

Yelena stood, watching helplessly for a moment as she saw Lara's skin begin to glow and shimmer with silver scales, her eyes unrecognisable and golden. She rushed forward as Lara's back arched suddenly, large silver-scaled wings erupting from her back.

"It's alright Lara... it's all going to be alright..." Yelena whispered as she watched Lara helplessly.

They all stood back as Lara rose a few feet in the air, her powerful wings beating so fast they didn't seem to be moving at all. Her face had elongated slightly and she was now entirely covered in pearly silver scales, except for her golden black tail. She turned to Yelena.

"What is happening to me? What am I?" she said in a deep voice not her own, flames still flickering on her body.

Yelena looked at her sadly. "Lara, I have kept something from you all these years... we wanted to protect you. That is why we told you that you were fey... they would have hunted you down if they had known the truth... Lara you're a dragon—in fact you are the last dragon."

***

Elsewhere, two women watched the events unfolding.

"So it is done," the tall blonde said.

The redhead nodded. "It was time. She had chosen."

"The Tallan accepted her readily," Asena turned to Caliana. "I have never seen it take to one so willingly..."

Caliana nodded. "It recognised her, my lady. It recognised her essence and deemed it worthy."

Asena sighed. "I know Yelena wanted to delay this moment for as long as she could... but what is done is done. Now that Lara knows the truth our vow of silence is ended Caliana. We must train Lara and guide her. I only pray that Lara is ready for what is to come."

Caliana nodded, "I hope we all are my lady. There are darks days ahead for us all."

ABOUT THE AUTHOR

Ela Lourenco lives in Scotland with her two daughters and husband. She has been an avid reader since childhood and has long enjoyed mysteries, mythology and anything related to the paranormal/supernatural/mystical/science fiction. She loves nothing more than making up stories about faraway people and places (helped somewhat by a mind that just won't grow up!). When she isn't nose deep in a book or writing herself she can be found dancing around the kitchen whilst baking. Her biggest wish in life is to infect others with a passion for reading.

Made in the USA
Charleston, SC
07 December 2015